WEST

CARYS DAVIES

GRANTA

St Helens
Libraries

3 8055 25004 2425

Askews & Holts | 09-May-2019

AF | £8.99

...enue, London W11 4QR

...y Granta Books, 2018
...by Granta Books, 2019
...by Scribner, an imprint of Simon
...ew York

...Carys Davies

...ed as the author of this work
has been asserted by her in accordance with the Copyright, Designs
and Patents Act, 1988.

All rights reserved. This book is copyright material and must not be copied,
reproduced, transferred, distributed, leased, licensed or publicly performed or
used in any way except as specifically permitted in writing by the publisher, as
allowed under the terms and conditions under which it was purchased or as
strictly permitted by applicable copyright law. Any unauthorized distribution
or use of this text may be a direct infringement of the author's and publisher's
rights, and those responsible may be liable in law accordingly.

This book is a work of fiction. Any references to historical events, real people,
or real places are used fictitiously. Other names, characters, places, and events
are products of the author's imagination, and any resemblance to actual events
or places or persons, living or dead, is entirely coincidental.

A CIP catalogue record for this book is available from the British Library.

1 3 5 7 9 10 8 6 4 2

ISBN 978 1 78378 423 3 (paperback)
ISBN 978 1 78378 424 0 (ebook)

Interior design by Jill Putorti

Offset by Avon DataSet Ltd, Bidford on Avon, B50 4JH

Printed and bound by CPI Group (UK) Ltd, Croydon, CR0 4YY

www.granta.com

MIX
Paper from
responsible sources
FSC® C020471

for C, G, B & A

From what she could see he had two guns, a hatchet, a knife, his rolled blanket, the big tin chest, various bags and bundles, one of which, she supposed, contained her mother's things.

"How far must you go?"

"That depends."

"On where they are?"

"Yes."

"So how far? A thousand miles? More than a thousand miles?"

"More than a thousand miles, I think so, Bess, yes."

Bellman's daughter was twirling a loose thread that hung down from his blanket, which until this morning had lain upon his bed. She looked up at him. "And then the same back."

"The same back, yes."

She was quiet a moment, and there was a serious, effortful look about her, as if she was trying to imagine a journey of such magnitude. "That's a long way."

"Yes, it is."

"But worth it if you find them."

"I think so, Bess. Yes."

He saw her looking at his bundles and his bags and the big tin chest, and wondered if she was thinking about Elsie's things. He hadn't meant her to see him packing them.

She was drawing a circle in the muddy ground with the toe of her boot. "So how long will you be gone? A month? More than a month?"

Bellman shook his head and took her hand. "Oh, Bess, yes, more than a month. A year at least. Maybe two."

Bess nodded. Her eyes smarted. This was much longer than she'd expected, much longer than she'd hoped.

"In two years I will be twelve."

"Twelve, yes." He lifted her up then and kissed her forehead and told her goodbye, and in another moment he was aloft on his horse in his brown wool coat and his high black hat, and then he was off down the stony track that led away from the house, already heading in a westerly direction.

"Look you long and hard, Bess, at the departing figure of your father," said her aunt Julie from the porch in a loud voice like a proclamation.

"Regard him, Bess, this person, this fool, my brother, John Cyrus Bellman, for you will not clap eyes upon a greater one. From today I am numbering him among the lost and the mad. Do not expect that you will see him again, and do not wave, it will only encourage him and make him think he deserves your good wishes. Come inside now, child, close the door, and forget him."

For a long time Bess stood, ignoring the words of her aunt Julie, watching her father ride away.

In her opinion he did not resemble any kind of fool.

In her opinion he looked grand and purposeful and brave. In her opinion he looked intelligent and romantic and adventurous. He looked like someone with a mission that made him different from other people, and for as long as he

was gone she would hold this picture of him in her mind:
up there on his horse with his bags and his bundles and his
weapons—up there in his long coat and his stovepipe hat,
heading off into the west.

She did not ever doubt that she would see him again.

John Cyrus Bellman was a tall, broad, red-haired man of thirty-five with big hands and feet and a thick russet beard who made a living breeding mules.

He was educated, up to a point.

He could write, though he spelled badly. He could read slowly but quite well and had taught Bess to do the same.

He knew a little about the stars, which would help when it came to locating himself in the world at any given moment. And should that knowledge ever prove too scanty or deficient, he had recently purchased a small but, he hoped, reliable compass, which he showed to Bess before he left—a smooth, plum-sized instrument in a polished ebony case, which when the time came, he promised, would point him with its quivering blue needle, home.

A week ago he had ridden out to his sister, Julie's, and stood on her clean scrubbed floor, shifting his weight from one large foot to the other while she plucked a hen at the table.

"Julie, I am going away," he'd said in as bold and clear a voice as he could muster. "I would appreciate it if you'd mind Bess a little while."

Julie was silent while Bellman reached inside his coat and took from his shirt pocket the folded newspaper cutting, smoothed it out, and read it aloud, explaining to his sister what it was he intended to do.

Julie stared at him a moment, and then flipped the hen onto its back and resumed her plucking, as if the only sensible thing now was to pretend her big red-haired brother hadn't spoken.

Bellman said he'd try to be back in a year.

"A *year?*"

Julie's voice high and strangulated—as if something had gone down the wrong way and was choking her.

Bellman looked at his boots. "Well, possibly a small fraction more than a year—but not more than two. And you and Bess will have the house and the livestock and I will leave the clock and Elsie's gold ring for if you ever get into any sort of difficulty and need money, and Elmer will lend a hand with any heavy work, I'm sure, if you give him a cup of coffee and a hot dinner from time to time." Bellman took a breath. "Oh, Julie, please. Help me out here. It's a long way and the journey will be slow and difficult."

Julie started on another hen.

A blizzard of bronze and white feathers rose in a whirling cloud between them. Bellman sneezed a number of times and Julie did not say, "God bless you, Cy."

"Please, Julie. I am begging you."

"No."

It was a lunatic adventure, she said.

He should do something sensible with his time, like going to church, or finding himself a new wife.

Bellman said thank you but he had no interest in either of those suggestions.

The night before his departure, Bellman sat at the square pine table in his small, self-built house drinking coffee with his neighbor and sometime yard hand, Elmer Jackson.

At ten o'clock Julie arrived with her Bible and her umbrella and the small black traveling bag that had once accompanied her and Bellman and Bellman's wife, Elsie, across the Atlantic Ocean all the way from England.

Bellman was not yet entirely packed, but he was already dressed and ready to go in his brown wool coat and a leather satchel across his front on a long buckled strap. A new black stovepipe hat sat ready on the table next to his big clasped hands.

"Thank you for coming, Julie," he said. "I am very grateful."

Julie sniffed. "I see you still intend to go."

"I do, yes."

"And where is your poor soon-to-be-orphaned little girl?"

Bess, said Bellman, was asleep in her bed over there in the corner behind the curtain.

He asked Julie if she would like coffee and Julie said she supposed she could drink a cup.

"I was just telling Elmer here, Julie, about the route I plan to take."

Julie said she wasn't interested in his route. Julie said why did men always think it was interesting to discuss directions and the best way to get from A to B? She leaned her umbrella against the wall, laid her Bible on the table, and sat down in front of her coffee, took a stocking out of her black traveling bag and began to darn it.

Bellman leaned in a little closer towards his neighbor.

"You see, Elmer, I've been looking at some maps. There aren't many, but there are one or two. At the subscription library over in Lewistown they have an old one by a person called Nicholas King and a not so old one by a Mr. David Thompson of the British North West Company, but they are both full of gaps and empty spaces and question marks. So on balance I think I'm better off relying on the journals of the old President's expedition, the one undertaken by the two famous captains—they're full of sketches and little dotted trails that show the best way through the tangle of rivers in the west and also the path over the Stony Mountains to the Pacific Ocean, should I need to continue that far."

Elmer Jackson belched softly. He looked up from his coffee with watery, bloodshot eyes. "What expedition? What famous captains?"

"Oh, Elmer, come now. Captain Lewis and Captain Clark. With their big team of scouts and hunters. They journeyed all the way to the Pacific Ocean and back at the old President's bidding. You don't recall?"

Elmer Jackson shrugged and said maybe he did, he wasn't sure.

"Well they did, Elmer. Seven thousand miles, two and a half years, there and back, and I'm thinking my best bet is to follow the path they took, more or less, and then diverge from it here and there, to explore where they didn't, in the hope that I can find my way to what I'm looking for."

"Diverge?"

Julie made an irritated, tsking sound with her tongue, and Jackson belched softly a second time. Bellman rubbed his big hands together. His face was pink with enthusiasm and excitement. He reached for a pickle jar from the shelf above Jackson's head.

"Imagine, Elmer, that this pickle jar is this house, here in Pennsylvania."

He set the jar in front of Jackson, at the far right-hand edge of the table. "And over here—if I might commandeer your coffee cup, Elmer, for a moment—is the town of St. Louis."

He set down Jackson's coffee cup a little to the left of the pickle jar.

"From where we are now"—he tapped the pickle jar—"to St. Louis"—he tapped the coffee cup—"is about eight hundred miles."

Elmer Jackson nodded.

"And way over here"—Jackson's watery, bloodshot eyes followed Bellman's hands as they lifted his tall new hat into a position over on the far left edge of the table—"are the Stony Mountains, also known as the Rocky ones.

"So. All that's needed is for me to travel first to St. Louis, where I will cross the Mississippi River and from there"—he began walking his fingers in a long arc that started at the coffee cup and curved up and across the large and vacant space in the middle of the table in the direction of the hat—"I will follow the Missouri River, as the two captains did, towards the mountains."

Elmer Jackson observed that relative to the eight hundred miles between the pickle jar and the coffee cup, the journey along the Missouri looked to be a big one.

"Oh it is, Elmer, yes. A very big one. I reckon about two thousand miles. Except it will be longer, because as I said, I will be *diverging*. Yes I will. I'll be straying from it quite a bit as I go along so I can have a look in some of the big empty areas the two captains didn't get to."

Jackson, whose own forty-year-old life so far had been a slow, meandering, and sometimes circular journey via a succession of gristmills, foundries, breweries, and a stint of soldiering, let go of a long whistle. He told Bellman he'd never taken him for such an adventurer. "And after the hat?"

"After the hat, Elmer, there's a longish run down to the Pacific Ocean, but I'm hoping I won't need to go that far. I'm hoping that if I don't find what I'm after near the river, then they'll be here, before the mountains"—his big hands circled the open expanse of table—"somewhere in this large, unknown interior territory."

Elmer Jackson scratched his belly and helped himself to another cup of Bellman's coffee and announced that he couldn't think of a single thing that would convince him to pitch *his* ass halfway across the entire goddamn earth.

Julie said she would thank Elmer Jackson not to curse.

Julie said, "Has it not occurred to you, Cy, that there will be savages?"

The savages he would encounter, said Julie, would be sure to set upon him the moment they spied his bright red hair and big, lumbering, foreign shape approaching them through the wilderness.

Bellman said he hoped not.

Bellman said from what he'd read the Indians where he was going were very content so long as you had a supply of useful manufactured objects and a handful of trinkets to give them, and he was bringing a fair few of those with him.

Jackson raised a hairy eyebrow and said he'd met as many Indians here in the United States as he hoped to in one lifetime and there was nothing would tempt *him* to run the gauntlet of all those gaudy painted faces and seminaked bodies in any kind of hurry.

Bellman nodded. He smiled in his genial way and patted the handle of his knife and the upward-pointing barrel of the rifle that stood propped against the table.

"I'll be fine, Elmer. Don't you worry."

Julie pressed her lips together, shook out the stocking in her lap, and said she didn't understand why a person would travel three thousand miles in an opposite direction from his home and his church and his motherless daughter. "No good father, Cy, would leave his flesh-and-blood child for such foolishness."

Elmer Jackson chortled. He seemed to find the back-and-forth between brother and sister a great entertainment.

Bellman let go of a long breath. "Oh, Julie—"

"Don't Oh-Julie me, Cyrus."

Bellman sighed. There was a helpless look about him. "I have to go. I have to go and see. That's all I can tell you. I have to. I don't know what else to say."

"You could say you're not going."

With one of his large and pawlike hands Bellman reached out to his sister across the table. Quietly, almost reverently, and with a kind of childlike wonderment, he said, "If they are out there, Julie, then I will be the one to return with news of their existence. Wouldn't that be a great thing?"

Julie laughed. "It would be a great thing, Cy, if you'd leave me and Bess with more than an old clock and a gold ring and a farmyard of miserable animals—one ancient stallion and a trio of exhausted mares, a clutch of jacks and jennies, a few unsold hinnies, and one bad-tempered molly mule."

Elmer Jackson drank the last of his coffee and stood up grinning. He rubbed his hand across his belly and stretched and announced that it was past his bedtime. On his way out he slapped Bellman on the shoulder and said to Julie if she ever needed a hand with the mules, just give him a holler.

When morning came Bellman was kneeling on the patched and sloping porch, arranging the bags and bundles he was taking with him.

Why, asked Bess, was he taking her mother's blouse?

Elsie's pink and white striped blouse lay across Bellman's big hands as he considered which bag to put it in.

"For the same reason, Bess, that I am taking her thimble and her knitting needles."

"And why is that?"

Bellman hesitated. He looked at his hands. "Because she does not need them anymore and I do."

He told her, then, about the Indians—how fond he'd heard they were, the men and the women both, of pretty pieces of clothing and useful metal items. One of them would be very attracted to her mother's blouse, others to her long steel knitting needles and her copper thimble. They would give him all sorts of things in return that he would need in the course of his journey.

"What kind of things?"

Bellman shrugged. "Food. Maybe a new horse if I need one. The knowledge of how to do things and which way it will be best for me to go."

Bess looked at him gravely and nodded. "Perhaps they can tell you where to look?"

"Exactly."

He showed her then a tin chest full of trinkets that would go with him along with her mother's things. Bess looked inside and saw that it was full of buttons and beads and bells, some fishhooks and some tobacco and scraps of ribbon and pieces of copper wire and a pile of handkerchiefs, a few short lengths of colored cloth, and small fragments of mirror glass.

Bess said she hoped the Indians would be pleased with them and Bellman said he hoped so too.

He would write to her, he said, and whenever he could, he'd give the letters to traders or travelers who'd bring them back east to somewhere like St. Louis or St. Charles and send them on.

"Look, I even have a little inkwell here on a spike behind the lapel of my coat. I won't even have to stop to write you a letter—I can write to you from my saddle as I'm going along."

The whole thing had lit a spark in him.

For half a day he'd sat without moving.

He'd read it a dozen times.

When Bess came in from the yard wanting to chatter and play, he'd told her to run along, he was busy.

When darkness fell he lit the lamp and read it again. He fetched a knife and scored it around and folded it into quarters and placed it in the pocket of his shirt, next to his heart. He felt his breath come differently. He could no longer sit still. He paced about and every half hour he took the folded paper from his shirt pocket and smoothed it flat on top of the table and read it again: there were no illustrations, but in his mind they resembled a ruined church, or a shipwreck of stone—the monstrous bones, the prodigious tusks, uncovered where they lay, sunk in the salty Kentucky mud: teeth the size of pumpkins, shoulder blades a yard wide, jawbones that suggested a head as tall as a large man. A creature entirely unknown. An *animal incognitum*. People poking and peering at the giant remains and wondering what had happened to the vast beasts the bones had belonged to. If, perhaps, the same gigantic monsters still walked the earth in the unexplored territories of the west.

Just thinking about it had given him a kind of vertigo.

For months, he thought about nothing else. When Bess came asking if he wanted to play checkers or go for a walk outside to pet the new hinny with a white patch on its face, he said no. For several weeks he spent most of his days in bed. When he did drag himself to his feet he worked mechanically in the yard and pasture with the animals, and when the new mules and hinnies were born he went to town and sold them. When a winter storm took off half the roof, he repaired it. He cooked, and occasionally he cleaned, and made sure Bess had a pair of shoes on her feet, but he was silent the whole time and sometimes his eyes turned glassy and he would not let Bess come near him. The giant beasts drifted across his mind like the vast creature-shaped clouds he saw when he stood in the yard behind the house and tipped his head up to the sky. When he closed his eyes, they moved behind the lids in the darkness, slowly, silently, as if through water—they walked and they drifted, pictures continually blooming in his imagination and then vanishing into the blackness beyond it, where he could not grasp them, the only thing left in his head the thought of them being alive and perambulating out there in the unknown, out there in the west beyond the United States in some kind of wilderness of rivers and trees and plains and mountains and there to behold with your own two eyes if you could just get yourself out there and find them.

There were no words for the prickling feeling he had that the giant animals were important somehow, only the tingling that was almost like nausea and the knowledge that it was impossible for him, now, to stay where he was.

Before the summer was over he was standing in his sister's house.

"All I can say, Julie, is that they feel very real to me. All I can say is that the only thing in the world I want to do now, is to go out there, into the west, and find them."

From Lewistown, Bellman proceeded through small towns and settlements along roads, which, though rough and broken for long stretches, brought him slowly further and further west. When he could, he bought himself a bed and dinner and sometimes a bath, but mostly he fished and hunted and picked fruit and slept out under his blanket. Arriving at the steep up-and-down of the Alleghenies, he did his best with his compass and his eye on the sun, and while he lost himself many times on the pathless slopes and along narrow tracks that led into the trees and then nowhere, here he was now, crossing from the east to the west side of the Mississippi on the ferry, which was a narrow canoe called a pirogue. His horse and his gear made the crossing on two pirogues lashed together with a wooden plank on top. The whole thing bumped twice against the landing and then it was still.

He was a little afraid.

The reason he'd decided to buy the black stovepipe hat at Carter's in Lewistown instead of staying with his old brown felt one was that he thought he would cut a more imposing figure in front of the natives here, beyond the frontier; that they would think of him, if not as a king or some kind of god, then at least as someone powerful who was capable of doing them harm.

And as the months passed and he followed the Missouri River while it meandered north and west, and he encountered various bands of Indians, traded with them and had no trouble, he came to think that the hat had been a good choice and to consider it a kind of talisman against danger.

In St. Louis he'd stopped for half a day and bought two kettles, one for his own use and one to trade; more handkerchiefs and cloth and buckles and beads—all these to trade too, and with each new group, he exchanged his bits and pieces for things to eat. Then he drew a picture on the ground of how he imagined the great beasts might look, trying to convey the animals' enormous size by pointing to the tops of available trees, pine or spruce or cottonwood or whatever happened to be nearby, but always the natives pulled a face that gave him to understand, no, they had seen nothing like the things he was looking for.

Bellman nodded. It was what he'd expected: that he had not yet come far enough; that he would need to go much deeper into the unorganized territories.

Slowly he traveled overland, not so far from the river as to get lost, but far enough that he had an opportunity to scour the occasional spinney of trees or forest or look out across the open ground or wander up and along some of the smaller streams and creeks.

Sometimes, in the thickest parts of the forest, he left the horse tethered and proceeded on foot for a day at a time, clambering over rocks and up and down gullies, splashing through mud and water, and returning exhausted in the evenings.

Every few weeks he looped back to the river in the hope of hitching a ride on one of the bateaux or mackinaws the traders used, making their slow and arduous journey upstream, and once or twice, he was lucky.

✦

True to his word, Bellman wrote to Bess as he rode along, dipping his pen into the pool of ink in the metal container speared through the lapel of his coat. He also wrote to her standing aboard the low, flat rivercraft on which he occasionally managed to hitch a ride, or in the evenings in front of his fire before he wrapped himself in his big brown coat and his blanket and pulled his black hat over his eyes and went to sleep.

Over the course of the first twelve hundred miles of his journey he wrote some thirty letters to his daughter and gave them, in four small packages, into the hands of people he met who were heading in the opposite direction: a soldier; a Spanish friar; a Dutch land agent and his wife; the pilot of a mackinaw he passed as it made its way downstream.

The weeks passed and he shot plover and duck and squirrel and quail.

He fished and he picked fruit and he ate quite well.

He was full of hope and high spirits, and there were times while he was going along when he couldn't help calling out over the water or up into the trees, "Well this is fine!"

Then winter came, and it was harder than he'd thought possible.

Long stretches of the river froze and Bellman waited, hoping to see one of the low, flat boats heading upstream, breaking apart the ice with poles, but there were none.

He met a small party of Indians, four men and a woman and a girl, who swapped some dried fish and a bag of corn mixed with sugar for one of his small metal files, but that was all. The large bands of natives he'd come upon earlier seemed to have vanished.

The days were very dark. He was cold and wet to the skin; the freezing rain ran down inside his soaking garments. His big squelchy coat was heavy as a body and there were times when he wondered if he'd be better off without it. Every few hours he wrung it out and water gushed onto the ground as it did from the pump at home, in surges.

Snow, then, cast itself over everything in deep drifts and an icy, unbroken crust formed on top of it. Bellman pressed on like a drunk, plunging and sometimes falling, the horse doing no better, both of them trembling and weak.

He had a little jerked pork and some of the Indians' dried fish, the bag of corn that he eked out a pinch at a time. Occasionally he trapped a bony rabbit, but mostly even the animals seemed to have disappeared. Soon his dinner was only a paste of leaves or a stew of sour grass dug out of the snow. He gnawed on frozen plant buds and bark and small twigs, and his horse did the same. His gut tightened with shooting pains, his gums were soft and bleeding. He slept in caves and hollow trees and under piled-up branches. Every day he expected his horse to die.

Once, he was sure he saw a band of figures in the distance, fifty or sixty strong, on horseback, moving through the falling snow. They seemed to be traveling quickly, at a loose, rapid trot, as if they knew some secret way of passing across the landscape that he didn't.

"Wait!" he called to them, but his voice came out like a rattle, a thin rasp that died on the cold wind, and the riders went on through the dusky whiteness until it covered them like a veil and they disappeared.

For a week he lay beneath his shelter and didn't move. Everything was frozen, and when he couldn't get his fire going he burned the last of the fish because it seemed better to be starving than to be cold.

And then one night he heard the ice booming and cracking in the river, and in the morning bright jewels of melting snow dripped from the feathery branches of the pines onto his cracked and blistered face, his blackened nose.

Later that day he caught a small fish.

Berries began to appear on the trees and bushes.

Winter ended and spring came and he continued west.

Through the thick cloth of the curtain in front of her bed, Bess had not been able to watch as her father described to Elmer Jackson and her aunt Julie the route he planned to take into the wilderness.

She had lain with her eyes open though, listening to him speak on the other side of the coarse, half-illuminated weave of the curtain, trying to picture for herself the hundreds and hundreds and hundreds of miles and all the difficulties and dangers and thrilling, exciting discoveries and new things he would come across between where she was now and where he was going.

After a month she asked her aunt Julie if they could go to the library so she could look at the big journals of the President's expedition and see the path her father had taken into the west, but Aunt Julie only looked at her in a kind of irritated amazement.

"And when, child," Bellman's sister demanded to know, "do you suppose I have time to sit in a library?"

On the banks of the Missouri River, Bellman made camp. The trees were thick with leaves, and there were tall grasses and flowers everywhere, purple, yellow, and white. One morning when he woke, a tall, sharp-featured man in a beaver hat stood over him and asked, "What brings you so far from home? Business or pleasure?"

From a pocket in his brown wool coat Bellman retrieved the folded and, by now, much worn newspaper cutting, and told the man in the beaver hat about the colossal bones that had been dug up in Kentucky. Bones, he explained, that were bleached and pale and vast, like a wrecked fleet or the parched ribs of a church roof. Bones that belonged to mammoth creatures that very possibly still existed beyond the United States and to this day roamed the prairies or the forests or the foot-hills of the great mountains in the west.

The man, whose name was Devereux, raised his dark and pointed eyebrows in amusement.

"Is that right?" he said, smiling.

"Yes, sir," said Bellman, "I think it might be." Devereux could not keep himself from laughing. He shook his head, chuckling, because he'd been trading furs in these parts for twenty-nine years, and in all that time, he said, he'd never seen anything bigger than a buffalo.

Bellman nodded cordially and observed that even the largest creatures are inclined to be shy, and almost all wild things consider it more sensible to remain concealed in the trees or bushes than to go parading themselves in the open.

Devereux laughed at that too—a picture in his head of the big monsters trying to hide behind a rock or a skinny pine tree.

He tapped Bellman on the knee with the end of his pipe. "Believe me, sir, you are on a hiding to nothing. A fool's errand. I would recommend at this point you turn yourself around and go home."

They were seated now on two logs outside the fur trader's shack. From a store of supplies arranged along two rough shelves inside, Bellman had purchased tobacco and a new pair of boots, a box of powder and ammunition, a bag of flour.

Bellman knew that the fur trader thought he was an idiot and a half-wit. He didn't mind. He'd met plenty of people since leaving Pennsylvania who thought the same thing.

The fur trader was chuckling again and talking now about the President's expedition, which had passed through this very spot not more than a dozen years ago. He was chuckling and saying that, if the big monsters were out there, you'd have thought the two intrepid captains and their men might have seen them. "All that way—you'd think they'd of got at least one tiny glimpse. The beasts being so large and all and difficult to miss."

Bellman shook his head. He smiled warmly and pulled the collar of his coat up around his big red beard and rubbed his large hands together in the chill morning air. He could not account for what the President's men had or hadn't seen. Nor could he explain why he himself felt so sure the monsters were out there. He could only say that what he'd read in the news-paper had produced a fierce beating of his heart, a prickling at the edge of his being, and there was nothing he wanted more now than to see the enormous creatures with his own two eyes.

Devereux tilted his head. He regarded Bellman's face in the dawn and seemed to regret having teased him. He punched him softly in the chest with his fist to show that he'd only been messing with him.

"You carry on, sir!" he said loudly with a large smile and a sweeping, encouraging gesture towards the western horizon. "What do I know? Who am I to say what might or might not be out there?"

He gave Bellman another soft punch and suggested a pirogue would be a good idea, and his own Indian, to take him up over the cataracts and generally help him through the river, which was a horrible stretch of water for at least the next three hundred miles. If it wasn't sluggish and shallow and strewn with timber and sandbars, it was boisterous and rough and would tip you out of the pirogue as soon as it would scoot you along a single yard in the direction you wanted to go. For a price, said the fur trader, he could procure him an Indian, and a second horse.

Indeed, he had the very person, he said. An ill-favored, narrow-shouldered Shawnee boy who bore the unpromising name of Old Woman From A Distance.

Winter came, then spring.

For a long time there was nothing but snow and then a greening began in the bare trees and the birds started to return. Elmer Jackson mended the fence on the south side of the yard and repaired the hen coop. He replaced four rotten planks on the porch and cleared a new area of pasture beyond the house, felling timber and removing stones from the ground. Aunt Julie washed all four of the small, square windows with vinegar, scrubbed and polished the pine table, and moved it to a new place on the opposite side of the room.

Bess waited for her father's letters but none came.

She helped her aunt with the mules and on Sundays she walked the hour and a half it took to get to church with her friend Sidney Lott, the two of them dawdling and talking behind Sidney's parents and sisters and Bess's aunt Julie. Bess spoke often of her father's absence, his long journey into the unknown.

There was a pleasure and a comfort in telling Sidney the same things over and over, and Sidney didn't seem to mind. He seemed happy to ask the same questions again and again and to listen to Bess give the same answers.

How many guns did he take?

Two.

How many knives?

One, I think.

Did he have any other weapons?

Yes, as far as I know, a hatchet.

Did he have any sort of map?

No. But he looked at some in the subscription library in Lewis-town before he left.

She told Sidney about the huge distances her father would now be covering along rivers and no doubt across prairies and probably over mountains. She also told him about all the haberdashery, decorative oddments, and assorted objects he had taken with him, which would be alluring to the Indians he'd be running into on his travels. With his bits and pieces, said Bess importantly, her father would be able to procure what he needed as he moved through the territory.

"He has taken my mother's blouse," she said, "because it is a beautiful item and he will be able to exchange it for a lot of stuff. Also her thimble, which is made of copper and has a pattern of flowers around it and is very pretty, and her knitting needles, which are long and sharp and made of steel and might therefore be considered very valuable and worth having."

The two children had this conversation many times, pretty much every Sunday over the course of several months.

Bess talked and Sidney nodded and contributed one of his occasional questions, until one Sunday morning Sidney expressed the opinion that Bess's father was an idiot and a half-wit and would never find what he was looking for.

Sidney said he didn't know a single person in Mifflin County who believed John Bellman would be successful in his mission, or that they would ever see him again.

From what he'd heard, said Sidney, Bess's father would be lucky to have got past St. Louis before being scalped and murdered by angry Indians, who would take a particular delight in getting their hands on his unusual bright hair and in carrying it, dripping blood, back to their rickety tents.

Bess's eyes smarted. She shouted at Sidney Lott. "You know nothing. You have no idea. You wait. You will see."

After that Bess did not talk to Sidney again and walked by herself on Sunday mornings to church, a long way behind the Lotts and her aunt Julie.

Rumors about Cy Bellman had begun to circulate soon after he started visiting the library and hinting at his plans to the new librarian there. When it became known that he'd actually left, everyone talked about his unusual quest and all agreed that it was insane, most people sharing the minister's opinion that very likely the bones in Kentucky would turn out not to be bones at all but ancient tree trunks and lumps of rock, others voicing the opinion that, even if the monsters were out there, it was surely not worth risking your life to find out.

Had Julie seen it coming? Helen Lott wanted to know. Had it been a surprise? Had she thought he'd do such a thing?

Cy, said Julie, had been acting strange for months before he left—either silent and morose and lost in thought, or jittery, endlessly talkative, practically *giddy*. But even then, she had not expected it. She'd heard about his rootling in the library, had picked up scraps of rumor and gossip, but Cy himself had not raised the subject with her and she'd kept herself quiet, thinking in time the whole thing would go away and come to nothing. You could have knocked her down with a feather that day in her kitchen when he'd finally told her outright what he was up to.

Helen Lott nodded. She'd seen similar behavior, she said, in other men of Cy's age.

"There's a childish dissatisfaction with everything they have, Julie, that reveals itself as they approach forty. It makes them think they deserve more than what life has served up to them. Mostly in my experience they take up with other women or buy themselves a new horse or a fancy hat."

Cy, said Julie, had never expressed interest in any other women after Elsie.

"He did buy himself a new hat though, from Carter's in Lewistown, before he left. A ridiculous tall city thing made of black shellac."

Helen Lott nodded wisely and with satisfaction, like someone who knew everything about everything.

Together, the two women proceeded towards the church.

Old Woman From A Distance was seventeen years old. He didn't much like his name but it had been given to him and for now it was his and he would put up with it until he got another.

In the end there hadn't been any kind of battle. In the end they had given in, succumbed, and agreed to take what they'd been offered and move off into the west.

Like a dark, diminished cloud, they had moved west across the landscape away from what had been theirs, eventually unpacking everything they'd been given for leaving, only to find they'd been given half of what had been promised.

It was all written out in the agreement with the amounts listed next to the items, but even before they met the English trader, Mr. Hollinghurst, and he told them what they had signed, the boy's people knew that what had been promised by the government's representative and what was written in the paper were not what they'd been given.

Of everything they'd been promised, they could see from the size of the bundles that there was less than half.

Half the money, half the red cloth, half the handkerchiefs, half the number of guns, half the powder, half the white ruffled shirts, half the blue jackets, half the rum, half the tobacco, half the white beads, half the red beads, half the blue beads, half the kettles, half the looking glasses, and so on and so on and so on.

Old Woman From A Distance remembered lying awake, listening to the men talk about what they should do. Some said they should go back and claim the rest of the things they'd been promised. Then one very old man said they should take nothing of what they'd been given—not a shirt, not a handkerchief, not a bead. He said that if they gave up their land for trifles, they would waste away.

He prophesied that a time would come when they would know that the whole of the earth had been pulled from beneath the skin of their feet, that they would wake up one morning in the dawn and find that all the forests and all the mountains, all the rivers and the vast sweep of the prairie, had slipped from their grasp like a rope of water, and all they had to show for the bargains they had made was some worthless jewelry, some old clothes, and a few bad guns. Everything they'd bartered—their dogs and their furs, their pounded fish and their root cakes, their good behavior, their knowledge of the country and the way they'd always done things—they would understand that they had given it all away for a song.

They would be driven to where the sun sets and in the end they would become quite extinct.

After that there was a silence, and after that more talking, all through the night. Old Woman From A Distance heard them speaking about the time the settlers had attacked them that past winter, how they'd gone after them and hunted them but had not succeeded because the settlers were more numerous and had better guns.

As dawn began to break, he heard his father say that there would always be more and more settlers, that for every one you saw, there were a hundred more coming behind him.

Eventually Old Woman From A Distance had fallen asleep, and when he woke it had been decided: they would keep what they'd been given by the government's representative even though they'd been cheated.

They would not go back and fight again.

They were tired and they were hungry. They would move west as they'd been told to and as they'd agreed they would, and on the new strip of land they'd accepted in exchange for their old ones, they would see how they got on.

And that's what they'd done. They'd packed up their tents and their dogs and their babies and their grandmothers, and in spite of the big cheating paper they'd continued west as they'd promised they would, moved off across the river, and kept going.

Old Woman From A Distance hadn't known what to think.

Part of him thought of his sister, and everything else they'd left behind in the east—their rivers and their forests and their neat gardens of beans and corn—and about the old man's prediction that if they took the things they'd been given in exchange, it would be the beginning of their end.

But another part of him coveted the things they'd been given, and this other part of him thought that the best they could do was to not regret all they'd lost. This other part of him thought that the business his people had entered into since they'd arrived in the west, with the Frenchman called Devereux and his partner, Mr. Hollinghurst, was on the whole a good thing rather than a bad thing.

He'd hesitated when Devereux had said to him one day, a piece of copper wire and a string of beads curled in his white palm like a short red snake, "Here, for that nice little pelt you have there."

How could you know the best thing to do? How could you know the future you would make with what you did now?

He wasn't sure. For a long moment he'd looked at the trader's outstretched hand and paused. Then he'd held out the pelt to Devereux and taken the wire and the beads, and when Devereux and the Englishman, Mr. Hollinghurst, had headed off to pursue their business further along the river, he'd made up his mind to go with them, away from his father's resignation and his mother's sorrow. He'd been Devereux's messenger and dogsbody ever since, keeping himself close to the trader, because even though he wasn't sure, it seemed like the best you could do.

Now, when the Frenchman brought him to meet the big redheaded white man, he stood and he looked and he listened while the two of them spoke together in a language he didn't understand but which he thought from the sound of it was the same or nearly the same as Mr. Hollinghurst's.

"Well?" said the fur trader, turning to him and speaking to him in his own tongue so he could follow, telling him there was profit in it.

For a few more moments the small, bowlegged Shawnee boy stood before the unusual stranger and thought about it all. About the profit that was in it. About the old man's warnings and his predictions, about his sister and everything else they'd lost.

He paused, looking at the man's red hair, turning it all over in his mind, and then he said yes.

If the big red-haired man paid him, he'd go with him.

Aunt Julie said it was disloyal and inconsiderate and unchristian of Bess to turn her back on Sidney Lott and refuse to walk with him any longer to church.

It was also a significant embarrassment, said Aunt Julie, when she herself still walked with the Lotts, who were important people. Every hundred yards or so now, on a Sunday, Helen Lott remarked that Bess, these days, seemed to think herself too good for Sidney. Sidney, who, said Aunt Julie, was a very nice boy and would soon be a fine young man.

When Bess remained silent, Aunt Julie predicted that the day would come when Bess would be very sorry for her rude behavior, but it would be too late then. It would be too late to be sorry when it was Sidney Lott who was the one to decide he had better things to do than keep *her* company on the long walk to church on a Sunday, or on any walk at all on any day of the week. It would be too late when he was the one to look right through her as if she wasn't there, and how would she feel when that happened?

Bess said she wouldn't care, she hated Sidney Lott. She preferred to walk by herself.

There were no books in the house except for her aunt Julie's Bible; the borrowed primer her father had used to teach her to read had long ago been returned to the schoolmaster in Lewistown. Bess's days were long and empty. A great part of them seemed to be taken up with listening to her aunt Julie talk about all the many things she had to do, and about the various things in the world she didn't like, such as venison, turnips, horses, donkeys, mules, and Roman Catholics. Bess did her chores, and when they were done she played checkers with herself or went for walks with her favorite hinny and wished that, like Sidney Lott, she went to school.

In the evenings she sat on the porch looking out along the stony track towards the west, and one day at the library in Lewistown when Aunt Julie was taking a seedcake to a woman with a broken hip, Bess asked a fat man in a yellow vest with a pair of eyeglasses on his nose if it was possible to peruse the volumes of the President's expedition into the west and he said, yes, if she was a subscriber. If she was a subscriber she could peruse all the books she liked. All she had to do was pay the subscription, which was nine shillings annually.

Behind him Bess could see the rows upon rows of books in their glass cabinets, and tables at which you could sit and read them. There were people there now.

Nine shillings.

The night before her father's departure she'd lain in her narrow bed behind the curtain and heard him at the table telling Aunt Julie there was the clock, and her mother's gold ring if they ever needed money. She looked past the man with the eyeglasses at the rows of books, their dark spines, and wondered which were the right ones. She wanted so much to see the maps and the rivers and the places where the huge animals might be and where her father might be now too, and then to

see which route he might follow on his return and to be able
to hold in her head a picture of him as he traveled home. She
tried to think of a way Aunt Julie wouldn't notice if the clock
or the gold ring were missing, but she couldn't. The clock
on the wall was the first thing you saw when you stepped in
the house, and she didn't know where the ring was kept. Her
father had worn it on a string beneath his shirt.

The man with the eyeglasses was looking down at her from
above his tall desk. She was old enough to know that the best
thing to do when you wanted something very much was to
pretend that you didn't. She turned and began to walk away,
doing her best to appear dignified and nonchalant. Even so,
she was fairly sure he was laughing at her when he called after
her, did she think she had the money for a subscription?

No, said Bess, she didn't.

The anniversary of her father's departure came and went, and
Bess turned eleven. Winter came again, and she pictured him
returning with a vast furry pelt big enough to carpet their
entire house, warm under their feet; people like her aunt Julie
and Sidney Lott and the fat librarian with the eyeglasses all
wishing they had one like it themselves.

For a long time snow lay in drifts around the house and
fell in wet flakes on the animals in the pasture. The cold iced
the windows on the inside and Bess made holes in it with her
warm breath so she could look out. Every day she hoped for a
letter but none came.

Not having Sidney anymore as a friend, she spoke to few
people aside from her aunt and their neighbor, Elmer Jackson,

when he came sometimes to lend a hand with the mules and afterwards to eat the supper Aunt Julie cooked for him in the evenings in recompense for his labor.

As a result Bess was often alone, and in her solitude she acquired a habit of talking out loud to herself.

"In eight more months, we will have four new mules and it will be summer. The days will be long and light, the potato blossom will be out, and I will be twelve."

The letters, ah.

Thirty of them, folded and tied up with cord in four small packages and entrusted, at various intervals, to

a Dutch land agent and his wife

a soldier

a Spanish friar

the pilot of one of the rivercraft on which Bellman hitched a ride upriver.

All promised that when they next found themselves in St. Louis or St. Charles, they would send on the letters.

Perhaps, on the day the Dutch land agent and his wife crossed the Mississippi, one of the oarsmen was drunk. Or perhaps the wide, keel-bottomed craft bumped against a chunk of drifting ice, or perhaps the family crowded in the bottom with their children and their cart and their two horses and their cow all moved over onto the same side suddenly and unbalanced it. Anyway, the ferry (which was a brand-new one built by Messrs. McKnight and Brady, merchants in St. Louis, who had purchased the old pirogue operation and replaced it with a new one not long after Cy Bellman had passed through earlier in the winter) yawed and tipped, and pretty much everything went into the water, including the Dutch-man's wife and the bag with Bellman's small pile of folded, tied-up letters. After that the freezing water washed off the ink in which he'd written Bess's name and a short misspelled paragraph describing the location of his house in Pennsylvania, and then the folded papers took in the cold water like a sponge until they grew heavy and found their way down to the riverbed and sank into the soft Mississippi mud.

The other losses were less dramatic, if no less accidental. One of the bundles sniffed out by a dog from the trouser pocket of the sleeping soldier; possibly the paper was scented with the pungency of one of Bellman's wood-smoked suppers. Anyway, it was eaten; the knotted twine, dripping with glistening dog slobber, all that remained when the soldier woke. The third was left by the Spanish friar at the post office in St. Louis and handed over the counter to a woman who came asking for mail. Her name was Beth Ullman; she put the letters in her bag and went on her way and did not return to rectify the mistake. The fourth, although delivered safely to the post office by the pilot of the mackinaw, fell out on the road after leaving St. Louis, bounced out of the carrier's loosely buckled bag on the way to Cincinnati and was lost.

All Bellman's letters to his daughter scattered like leaves across the soil and waters of the earth before she ever had a chance to read them.

Bellman had met many eccentrically named natives in the course of his long journey but none so peculiarly labeled as this one. Old Woman From A Distance was, he estimated, about sixteen years old, though it was hard to tell. With their smooth, beardless faces, even the older men looked young, and all of them, whatever their age, looked more or less the same to Bellman.

Devereux was right about the boy being not so well made as most of the others—he was barely five feet tall, his legs were bowed and rickety, and his eyes were very small, like pips, but he had a sharp, eager look about him, and according to the fur trader would be willing to barter his knowledge of the prairie, his skill with a pirogue, and his truffling after roots for a hand-kerchief or a bit of tobacco and a few worthless baubles that would glitter in the sunlight when it fell upon him through the willows.

He'd known the boy since he was a child, said Devereux. For seven years the boy had been running errands and taking messages for him, always quick, always eager and reliable. It would do him good now, a stint of scouting on his own account. He winked at Bellman. "Get him out from under my petticoats." He named a price in both dollars and shillings.

"Is he trustworthy?"

The fur trader grinned broadly and slapped Bellman on

the back. Everyone who passed through these parts always came asking him, sooner or later, about the Indians here—wanting to know their character, if they were the same as the ones that still lingered in the east, or different. "I always tell them the same thing"—Devereux rubbed his hands over the fire and invited Bellman to fill his pipe with more tobacco—"that they are generous and loyal, treacherous and cunning, as weak as they are strong and as open as they are closed. That they're shrewd and hopelessly naïve, that they are vengeful and mean and as sweet and curious as little children. That they are vicious killers. That they are terrible cooks and dancers. That if they have half a chance they'll keep a slave and torture him and when they're finished with him they're as quick as the next man to sell him to the highest bidder." The best thing, in his experience, that you could do, said Devereux, was to show them you had things they might want, and never startle them, in case they mistook you for some other breed of savage they didn't get along with. Further west, of course, if Bellman went far enough, he would come eventually upon the Sioux, who were ferocious regardless of who you were.

Bellman inclined his head. The smile between his red mustache and beard was polite but uncertain. He'd hoped for a more reassuring answer.

"But what about this one? Can I trust him?"

The fur trader stood up and stretched. "Oh, I'd say so, sir, yes, so long as you pay him for his services. For seven years, he's always done as he's been told."

With the fur trader's help Bellman explained to the boy what he was looking for.

Not wanting to waste his ink, he drew pictures with a stick

in the dust—how he theorized the creatures might look; how their horny skin or their fur or their coats of shaggy wool might cloak those enormous bones. He pointed to the top of the tallest cottonwood he could see, to indicate how large he believed they were. The boy looked at the pictures. The expression on his beardless face did not change, and he stood for a long time before he said something in his own language.

Bellman waited. "Well?"

Devereux flapped his hand. "He says he's never seen anything like that in his life. He'll go with you, though, if you pay him."

Bellman dug into the larger of his two bags, past the folded cotton of Elsie's blouse, and pulled out a length of green ribbon and a fishhook; from the tin chest he took a fragment of mirror glass and a double string of red beads, a smidgen of tobacco and a white handkerchief, and presented them to the boy, who took the things, immediately tied the green ribbon and the glass in one of his dark pigtails, hung the beads around his neck, and tucked the handkerchief in the waist of the little skin skirtlet that covered his private parts like a sporran. Then he looked at Bellman and held out his hand for more. Devereux rolled his eyes and chuckled, as if to say, "Whatever you offer them, they will always ask for more."

"He is after another ribbon from your big box of treasure there, sir, for his other pigtail," said the fur trader, pointing, "and another string of beads, the blue ones, which he prefers to the red." Bellman hesitated. It seemed to him the boy was being a little greedy now and taking advantage of him; he'd begun, in the year that had passed since he left home, to be anxious about his dwindling supplies as each bargain he'd struck with the natives along his way depleted the contents of his box. He had only a few oddments left now. Still, he was eager to be under way again, and he thought his affairs would probably go better if the Indian came along with him than if he didn't.

He picked out a white ribbon and the shortest string of blue beads he could find and gave them to the boy, who put them on straightaway and looked now, thought Bellman, happy as a girl.

Before they left, Bellman asked Devereux if he would please send on some letters for his daughter, who was ten years old, no, eleven and living at home with his sister, who could be difficult but underneath was a good person. He had left several letters, he said, in the course of the last year with various travelers and other people he'd met. He knew his daughter would be waiting for more. Would Devereux be sure to send these latest ones on?

Devereux said he would.

That first day, they started at dawn. Bellman and the two horses, his black one and the boy's brown one, walking on the bank, the boy and the gear in the pirogue. Later they swapped, the swap confirming what Bellman had suspected all through the earlier part of the day, that the boy was more dextrous by far than he was with the log boat, flicking the paddle and passing easily between the sandbars and the driftwood that crowded the sluggish and disappointing stream. When Bellman clambered in to take the boy's place and began attacking the shallow water with the paddle, the boat stayed in the same place, spinning in an endless circle.

Thrashing about in the river, Bellman could see the boy on the bank doubled over with laughter, and as the pirogue continued to spin, Bellman too began to laugh until he was too weak even to try to move off in the right direction. He held aloft the paddle and signaled to the boy.

"Here. You can have another go."

As dusk began to fall, Bellman congratulated himself on his new acquisitions: the boy, the brown horse, and the boat.

Back now on dry land, leading the horses, he lengthened his stride.

He marveled at the beauty of his surroundings: the pale gray ribbon of the river; the dark trees; in the distance the bright spread cloth of the prairie, undulating and soft; the bruised blue silk of the sky.

He felt lighter; more hopeful than he had for months that he was moving closer towards what he was looking for.

Spring came round again and Elmer Jackson managed a dinner or at least a cup of coffee three or four days a week over at Bellman's place.

He felt quite at home these days.

He'd got better at not using any curse words, and more than once at the end of a day's work with the mules or after he'd done various odd jobs around the place, Bellman's sister had followed up the plate of cold meat with a slice of ginger cake or a piece of apple pie.

Ever since his tall, big-footed neighbor had gone wandering off into the sunset, Jackson had gone over there many times to lend a hand, coming and going on his gray, white-tailed horse. "Thank you, Elmer," the aunt said when he came, and again when the work was done and she was giving him coffee at the end of the day and sometimes dinner and sometimes the cake too, or pie.

It had been a great moment for Elmer Jackson, the day he'd arrived in Mifflin County with enough money in his pocket—scraped and hoarded over the years of laboring in gristmills and foundries and breweries and the horrible nineteen months he'd spent in General Wayne's army in Ohio—to buy his own small piece of land. It was a great moment when, after all the hard days and miserable nights in a ceaseless string of leaky tents and cramped, malodorous bunkhouses and garrisons, he took possession of his own parcel of ground, to have and hold if he so wished, in perpetuity.

He'd always liked Bellman's place more though—had always preferred it to his own. The tall mule breeder had arrived a year after he had, and from the beginning he'd appreciated the warmth and the cleanliness and the little touches of beauty in the other man's house—the row of pickle jars on the shelf, the sparkling windows; later on, the bright quilt with its rainbow of colors on top of the little girl's bed.

His own home was a series of roughly interlocking logs and a plank floor. There were no adornments or soft touches, only his bed and a table and a chair, a bucket for his business during the night, which he took outside in the morning and poured on top of the beans he planted every year in the back.

It seemed more than possible to him now that his neighbor would never come home. It seemed more than possible that if he was careful and played his cards right, he might have something of a free hand around the place.

He'd heard mention of a gold ring. With the proceeds from a gold ring he might expand the mule business, add some improvements to the house, some smart new garments for himself. Bellman's hat had been a fine thing.

He knew that people in town looked down on him; that Carter watched him in his store as if he thought Elmer was getting ready to palm something the moment his back was turned. On the few occasions he'd turned up in church, the minister had viewed him from a distance with a look that said he'd rather not have him sit down in his greasy pants on any one of his straight-backed wooden benches. Well, they would all greet him with more respect when he was running Bellman's place.

He took another mouthful of the aunt's pie.

The girl seemed to grow taller every day. She had her crazy father's red hair, but mostly, in Elmer Jackson's opinion, she resembled the dead wife. The wife had been neatly made, and the girl was too, and she had the same straight back and brisk walk.

As far as Elmer Jackson was concerned he had a choice, the aunt or the girl, and he had never much fancied the aunt. The aunt, with her long, bony face and wrinkly stockings, was scarcely more appealing to Elmer Jackson than one of her brother's mules.

When the girl was small she used to sit on the fence while he worked with Bellman in the yard, swinging her legs in a pair of cotton britches. At the beginning he hadn't known the first thing about mules and she'd sung out the basics to him in a high kind of chant like a nursery tune.

A girl donkey is a jenny and a boy donkey is a jack.

A stallion crossed with a jenny makes a hinny and a mare crossed with a jack makes a mule.

A boy mule is called a john and a girl mule is called a molly.

A girl hinny is sometimes called a mare hinny and a boy hinny is sometimes called a horse hinny but mostly we just call them hinnies.

If you put a boy hinny with a girl hinny or a jack mule with a molly mule or a girl hinny with a jack mule or a boy hinny with a molly mule you almost never get anything. Hinnies and mules can't have children at least hardly ever which is why you have to do everything with the horses and the donkeys. The real name for a mule—laughing and jumping off the fence and skipping away—*is an ass.*

He could wait a few years, he supposed.

In a few years the aunt could pack herself off back to her own place and take her wrinkly stockings and her brown and white chickens with her.

But as Elmer Jackson sat at Cy Bellman's table finishing Julie's pie and contemplating his future, he found that he did not want to wait a few years.

Lately, he's taken to spying on her. The hour on a Friday when the crotchety aunt fetches the small tin tub down off its hook on the wall and has her strip and bathe. She is a perfect little thing—reminds him of milk, or cream, cooling in the shed, a silken chill when you dip your finger but a soft warmth inside. Oh dear God, for a taste. With his eye pressed to the gap between the timbers he holds his breath and watches, not touching himself so that the pleasure when it comes will be the greater. It becomes his ambition, his one goal. He begins to plot how he will achieve it, feeling every day that, with his helpfulness in the yard, his patience with the mules, his appreciation of the aunt's cooking, his acceptance into their midst, he is coming closer, each friendly favor a new stone making a path along a river that he is almost across; that he is just waiting now for his chance to make it happen.

The big white man always fell asleep before he did.

Wrapped in his thick woolen coat, he was always snoring within a short time. His breathing slowed and deepened, and after that his body twitched from time to time like a sleeping dog's, and the boy wondered what dreams he had.

He'd seen a red-haired white man once before, the day the settlers had come and set fire to his people's crops and tents. Smaller and thinner but with the same flame-colored beard and head hair, pulling his sister into the open, his sister kicking and scratching and crying out, the skinny white settler with his red hair and his red beard moving on her like a dog and then cutting her throat. In his dreams he still saw her kicking and scratching and heard her crying out. When he woke and saw the big white man near him, half his face covered in red hair like the other one—there were times when he almost gagged.

A beard of any color was a gross thing, an animal thing, that carried in its bristles the stink of food, sometimes crumbs and threads of actual food. But this one was worse because it was red like the other man's. Sometimes as he and the big explorer were going along, when they were lifting the pirogue or strapping the bags onto the horses, the big red beard brushed against his cheek and he retched. The smell, the picture in his head of the skinny white man from before.

Some nights Bellman woke in the dark, and when he opened his eyes the boy was looking at him. Over on the other side of their softly glowing fire, points of light popping in and out, the ash shifting as the sticks burned through and broke and quietly fell, when Bellman looked the boy was not asleep but lying there with his small piplike eyes white and wide open in the dark.

It made Bellman feel safe. The boy awake like that and alert, watching for danger that Bellman might not even know was there.

It could be a troublesome business, the stallion covering the jennies and the jacks covering the mares—her father and Elmer Jackson doing much hauling about and yelling, the animals running this way and that, but eventually it all got done, and a little less than a year later the mules and the hinnies came, curled in their slippery bags, then tottering about on spindly legs into the pasture.

These days, with her father gone, her aunt Julie and Elmer Jackson managed it between them, with Elmer Jackson doing most of the work, whipping and organizing the stallion and the jennies, the mares and the jacks, coaxing and bullying depending on which ones were being reluctant and which were not.

This did not happen on one particular day, but on different days according to which animals were being brought together. Her aunt Julie did her bit from the sidelines with the special "yip yip" call her father used for the business, though once the thing was started Bess noticed that her aunt generally found some other job that needed doing, like digging up a few potatoes or scrubbing a tub full of laundry or some other task that required her attention inside the house, and left Elmer to see it through.

Bess got to help with the birthing though. The pulling and sometimes the roping and the whispering of encouragement into the long ears of the jennies or the short ears of the mares.

It was a wonder and a mystery, Bess used to tell Sidney Lott before she stopped speaking to him, two different animals, horse and donkey, coming together to produce a different one, and such a fine one! Mule or hinny, it made no difference: the mule was an excellent animal. "Stronger than either a horse or a donkey. A mule will carry more, Sidney, and go farther, plus they have a good, stout, hoofy kick, and are much cleverer."

"Why don't you go on a mule?" was a question she'd asked her father in the days before he left on his journey once it became clear he planned to take his black horse.

"That's a good question, Bess," he'd said, "and I've thought about it: which would be better, horse or mule."

He'd actually considered taking both, he'd said—making himself into a kind of small traveling caravan with him riding the horse and his gear loaded onto the mule, but in the end he'd rejected the idea, it seemed too slow and cumbersome, and the best thing seemed to him to crowd all his equipment, along with himself, onto the horse.

Bess said if she was going, she reckoned she'd probably choose a mule.

"A horse will be quicker, Bess," he'd said gently, squeezing her hand because he could see her eyes had filled with water. "A horse is a swift animal. A little brainless, I grant you. But I will go faster, Bess, and come back sooner, on a horse."

The days passed, it rained a lot, and as he rode or walked, Bellman scanned the riverbank and the prairie beyond, and the lines of struggling pines in the distance on the summits of the hills. From time to time he sketched the unfamiliar rocks, the trees and shrubs and grasses, and pressed some of their leaves and stalks between the pages of his drawings, but mostly his head was full of the giant animals.

What did they eat?

Were they fond of meat, or plants?

Did they, like the wolves, stalk and partake of the buffalo?

Were they, in spite of their enormous size, fleet of foot? Or did they move slowly, gently, like the cloud-creatures that had drifted across his mind's landscape when he first stumbled upon the possibility of their existence?

Were they hunters or were they gatherers?

Did they use their enormous tusks to spear their prey, or did they reach up with their mouths into the trees and nibble walnuts?

Did they graze, as he and Old Woman From A Distance did, on serviceberries and chokecherries, on ripe grapes?

Did they also relish a beaver tail or a fresh catfish?

He was encouraged by the sight of other animals he'd never seen before in his whole life and stopped to sketch them too: oversized rabbits with ears the size of the big flat paddle the boy used to ferry the pirogue along the river; a fat little beast somewhere between a frog and a lizard with spines all over its body; an ugly bird with feathers covering half its legs like a pair of short trousers, pale, horrible naked skin between the feathers and its big clawed feet.

These strange and unfamiliar creatures gave Bellman hope and he pressed on.

Accompanied by the boy, he made excursions to the north and south in the hope of a sighting, returning after a few days to the river and moving along it for a day or two, then repeating the exercise. Excursion. River. Excursion. River. Excursion. This was his slow, meandering, laborious approach. Week by week, month by month, they crept west.

There were times when the ground beneath his feet seemed to tilt again; when he was unsteadied, the way he'd been that day at home when he'd read for the first time about the huge bones: when the thought of everything he didn't know had made him dizzy, when he knew he couldn't stay at home. He'd been completely unable to explain it to anyone, not to Julie, not to Elmer, not even to the new librarian, who'd helped him find the maps and the journals. Now he wondered if it was because it seemed possible that, through the giant animals, a door into the mystery of the world would somehow be opened. There were times, out here in the west, when he lay down at night and, wrapped in his coat, he'd look up at the sky, its wash of stars, gaze up at the bright, broken face of the moon and wonder what might be up there too—what he'd find if he could just devise a way of getting there to have a look.

Winter came again, and it was very hard. So much snow Bellman thought it would bury them, and even the boy was unable to conjure much in the way of food from the frozen world around them. On the bitterest nights it occurred to Bellman that the best thing they could do would be to lie close to each other for warmth, but he couldn't imagine doing such a thing—he and the boy wrapped up against each other inside his coat or the blanket. Even on the worst nights it seemed an impossible thing to propose, and the two of them lay apart in the ice-cold arms of the night. For long periods they couldn't travel, and sometimes Bellman feared he had come all this way only to go no further.

But then spring arrived again, and in the mornings they woke to clear skies above and the quiet river below and continued on their way.

He enjoyed the quiet company of the boy: his constant and predictable presence; the sight of him up ahead with his hand resting lightly on the short hunting bow he carried with him at all times. The bow amazed Bellman. It was so small and slight it looked to him like a child's toy, and after all this time it still astonished him, the way Old Woman From A Distance could shoot with it from his galloping horse and return, day after day, with dead things for the two of them to eat.

Mostly, it seemed to Bellman that they were getting along pretty well.

As far as he could tell, the boy was happy enough with the bargain they had struck in the presence of the fur trader, Devereux. At night, after they'd eaten, Bellman often saw him twirling the mirror glass in the firelight, or rearranging the ribbons and beads and the white handkerchief that together decorated his black hair and thin, rickety-legged body.

Bellman liked the evenings after the long days of traveling—

the quiet, almost domestic contentment, their things put away for the day, the plates scraped and rinsed in the river, the warm fire casting soft shadows on their camp. Sometimes the two of them spoke aloud after they'd lain down for the night, Bellman in his language and the boy in his, neither one knowing what the other was saying.

It was pleasant, thought Bellman, communing in this way, listening to words whose meaning you didn't understand; like listening to music. And on top of everything there was the boy's skill with his bow and arrow, and he was a good fisherman too. All in all, thought Bellman, they were doing all right. There was plenty of game and enough fish in the river to feed a city.

From her bed Bess heard her aunt Julie and Elmer Jackson talking.

They were drinking coffee. Every now and then she could hear the soft clunk of their cups on the table.

"Of course I think about him," her aunt Julie was saying. "I think about him reading in the newspaper about the possible existence of a large, big-toothed monster and saying to himself, 'Oh, I know what to do! Pack my bags and buy myself a big new hat and point myself immediately in its direction and ride two thousand miles towards it so I can be sure of stepping right into its jaws.'"

Her aunt had made her voice deep and stupid-sounding, and Bess heard Elmer Jackson let go of a hearty laugh. When she peeked out from behind the curtain in front of her bed, she saw him slap his thigh.

She also saw that his appreciation of her aunt Julie's imitation of her father had caused her aunt to blush.

Bess had never seen her aunt Julie blush before.

She watched her aunt pat the coil of grayish brown hair at the back of her head above the collar of her dress and tuck a stray wisp of it behind her ear.

She'd never heard her aunt so cozy with Elmer Jackson, the two of them sitting there in the lamplight, drinking their coffee, and she wondered if maybe her aunt Julie wasn't getting a little bit sweet on their neighbor, and he on her. She would never have expected it. It was the last thing she would have predicted—her aunt's growing warmth towards Elmer Jackson, a surprising thing she couldn't fathom or explain. She wondered if this was how it would be from now on: Elmer Jackson here in the house almost every evening, her aunt Julie sitting with him and talking to him, and laughing with him about her father and blushing when Elmer Jackson laughed too.

Bess retreated again behind her curtain and lay down.

After a little while she heard the scratch of Elmer Jackson's chair across the wooden floor and the closing of the door, and then there were the sounds of her aunt Julie rinsing the coffee cups in the pail and taking off her boots, the creak of her father's bed upstairs as her aunt climbed into it.

In the darkness and the quiet Bess could hear the ticking of the wall clock. When she closed her eyes she still saw a picture of what the clock looked like after her father had ridden away—when she'd turned at last to go back into the house, it had its arms flung out across its big round face, one pointing one way and one in the opposite direction, as if one hand was pointing west and the other east. In daylight, there was a different time she liked more than any other and she did everything she could to be in the house when it arrived: the time when the bigger of the two hands crept slowly through the 12 until it joined the smaller one, both of them pointing east.

She lay now with her eyes closed.

Today a crow had come into the yard, which meant her father had found the big animals and had begun his journey home.

Tomorrow, if she made it from the pump to the house

without slopping a drop of water over the lip of the bucket, it meant he was in good health.

If the white hawthorn came into flower before the beginning of May, that also meant he was in good health.

And if her aunt Julie was in a bad mood first thing in the morning, it meant he'd be back before her birthday.

She did this all the time now—daily, sometimes hourly, and always last thing at night before she went to sleep, marking time by accumulating signs of good luck in her father's favor.

On balance, of course, things tended to come out on his side, because Bess always weighted the odds in his favor by setting outcomes she had some power to influence, or at least knew were likely, such as walking very slowly and very carefully with the bucket from the pump to the house and not filling it too full in the first place, or seeing that by late April the hawthorn already showed every sign of coming into bloom very soon, or being able to rely with a fair degree of certainty on her aunt Julie being irritable when she woke up in the mornings.

Still, it was a comfort.

She drew her knees up to her chin and pulled the quilt around her shoulders. Beyond the curtain in front of her bed the clock ticked.

Two o'clock in the afternoon was the time Elmer Jackson usually made his appearance these days; nine or ten in the evening by the time he picked up his hat and said good night to Aunt Julie and climbed up on his gray, white-tailed horse, and left.

They stopped beneath a bluff of blue clay. In the evening some rain fell and Bellman shot a duck and the boy made a fire and they ate.

Bellman did not feel like a vain man. "I am not seeking any kind of glory," he said, because it was a habit, now, to talk to the boy in the evenings after they'd eaten, even though the boy didn't understand what he was saying.

Still, it would be quite a thing, he couldn't help thinking, to write to the newspaper when he got home, and sit across from Julie, and Elmer Jackson, and Gardiner and Helen Lott, and maybe Philip Wallace, the schoolteacher, and the helpful librarian, whose name he couldn't recall, and Bess, of course, and tell them all about the beasts he had found and seen with his own two eyes. It would be quite a thing to chat to them about the creatures' real-life teeth and tusks. About the kinds of sounds they made. About the scaly or shaggy magnificence of them, whichever it turned out to be. The wonder of it all.

There were nights too, when he thought of Elsie.

Elsie on the ship as they came into New Castle, hair blowing, big smile; lit up with hopefulness of what this new country would give them.

Elsie heading out to the pump from the house with the bucket for water. Her straight back and her brisk walk.

Elsie taking a bath next to the stove, the water he poured

from the ewer sliding like oil over her skin, jagged peaks and ripples beneath that were Bess moving around inside her.

Elsie sitting at the table with Bess on her knee, Elsie helping him clear the pasture of stones. Elsie upstairs after the terrible operation. Mr. Corless the barber lingering in the doorway and asking, eventually, for his money; saying he was sorry but even the best surgeon could have done no better.

Some nights in his dreams he was with her again in their bed, and he'd reach for her and wake up. When it happened it was so real he tried straightaway to go back to sleep so he could get inside the dream and experience it all again, be with her as he'd been in life.

And then there were the other nights, when he dreamed that she was in the house watching him packing and packing and packing for his journey, trying to be off—rolling and re-rolling his blanket and stuffing things into bags and dropping other things into the tin chest. He couldn't see her, but he knew she was there somewhere in the background, he could feel her watching him, and he was never able to get the packing done—there was always more needing to go in and somehow he hadn't started soon enough or left enough time. In his dream there was always a feeling that a deadline loomed, that there was a certain time by which he had to set off, otherwise he would never leave, and he was desperate, desperate, desperate to be on his way, hurrying and hurrying, but it never went any quicker and he could feel the possibility that he would ever begin his journey becoming smaller and smaller and draining away to nothing, and even in the dream he could feel his panic, the pounding of his heart, and when he woke the desperation was still wild inside him.

Beyond the quiet fire, though, the boy slept. His eyes were

closed. Bellman could see the gentle rise and fall of his chest.
Above them the willows swayed lightly in the evening breeze
off the river. Bellman's breathing calmed. It was all right. He
was here. He was on his way.

And then, an accident.

Bellman's blanket left behind at the place they'd camped
the night before, some distance from the river; a decision to
head back as quickly as possible downstream to retrieve it.

They heard the falls long before they reached them.

Water crashing, then, between the walls of the high-sided
canyon and into the narrowing throat of the river.

Bellman pointed to the bank and a possible way up over
the rocky cliffs to show that he thought they should carry the
pirogue round, but the boy made it clear that he was confident
about taking the little boat over the cataract. And Bellman
said, all right. Because he'd watched the boy now for thou-
sands of hours and it seemed that he could do anything he
wanted—that the narrow canoe would do whatever he asked
of it. But when the boy and the boat rose up on the foaming
water, Bellman saw the boat flip. He saw all his things fly
out through the foam. His tin chest thrown through the dark,
roiling water and the lid flipped open and everything in it
joining the river's roaring spume in its plunging fall.

At the bottom Bellman took hold of the tops of the boy's
arms and shook him. It was the first time he'd turned on him
in anger. He shouted at him and told him he was useless and
then he sat down hard on the bank to survey the wreckage of
their afternoon, and it turned out they'd lost almost nothing.

The pirogue was unbroken and the paddle was washed up in a cleft between the rocks a little further along. In the tranquil pool at the bottom of the falls, Bellman's things floated or twinkled beneath the water.

"Well," he said. "I suppose we've been lucky this time."

Together they gathered all Bellman's scattered possessions and spread the wet things on the tops of gorse bushes to dry. Everything else—his kettle, his weapons, et cetera—they brought up onto the rocks and narrow, shaley beach. He untied the oilskin that contained his gunpowder and opened it to the sun. Even his letters to Bess, bundled next to the oilskin, had survived with remarkably little damage—some blurring and splotching and brown tidemarks here and there when they were dried, but that was all. A little further on they came to their camp of the previous day, where Bellman's blanket lay waiting for them.

"I'm sorry," said Bellman quietly when evening came and they'd finished eating. "I didn't mean to shout. I know it wasn't your fault. I think I'm just feeling a little anxious and tired and worried about winter coming on again, and that we've come all this way without a single sighting."

Every time now, the aunt invited him to stay for supper. He spent the days clearing up the yard and the pasture, and foraging the animals, and in the evenings she gave him a plate of cold meat and a cup of hot coffee and a piece of cake or pie before he took himself off.

One night before the girl went to bed and the aunt's back was turned, he leaned across the table and drew a circle with his thumb on the back of her hand as it rested beside her plate. She gave him a straight look, but didn't seem to know quite what he was about, and the next moment the aunt was back in her place and the girl was being sent off to bed and he was giving his attention again to his dinner.

He excoriated himself afterwards. It seemed to him that he should not have attempted anything so halfhearted—that the element of surprise, when the right moment came, was important. "The last thing you want," he said to himself, "is for the aunt to be on the kee veev."

That same spring in Lewistown, Mary Higson, the black-smith's widow, turned thirty-nine.

She'd seen Cy Bellman go into Carter's one summer afternoon not long before he left and come out wearing a hat that surprised her. Not knowing anything yet about his plans, she was curious about what he might be up to. Whether he'd made some private decision to improve his appearance and this was the first public sign; whether, after a period of eight years since his wife's death, he was thinking it was time to take an interest in something apart from his little girl and the mules she saw him driving into town every season in his brown felt hat and a willow switch and a steady look on his face that always seemed to her to say, "My name is John Cyrus Bellman and this is my life. It is not what I'd expected but there you are, this is how it is."

He'd looked sweetly self-conscious, though, she thought, exiting the store that day, the hat very straight and somehow precarious on top of his thick red hair, as if he were performing some sort of dare, like walking a greasy pole balancing a lampshade on his head while everyone he'd ever known in his life waited and watched to see if he, or the hat, or both, would fall off.

For a while afterwards she thought it was possible he might call.

Several times she went to the door thinking she'd heard

a knock, only to find it was nothing and there was no one, it had been her own hoping and wishing, conjuring sounds out of silence or confusing something ordinary and haphazard like the plop of a large raindrop on the roof or a person in the street taking off a shoe and knocking it on the ground to empty it of a stone.

And then one day she heard in church that he'd ridden off by himself into the west to look for some extremely big animals.

She overheard his sister Julie and Helen Lott and the minister all talking about it, saying that no doubt the enormous objects that had inspired his search were likely not bones at all but bits of tree and rock. That he was crazy to go out there alone. That he would starve or break a leg or get lost or fall into the hands of savages.

She didn't know what to think, except that she wished he hadn't gone.

Every time she saw his little girl, whose hair was exactly the same red as his, she thought of him and her heart turned over.

She was a funny little thing, the girl.

Solitary and solemn and always trailing a long way behind her aunt and the Lotts on their way to church.

Sometimes the blacksmith's widow glimpsed her loitering on the library steps. Once, she saw her go in through the big wooden doors, and once she saw her fly out of them like a scalded cat straight into her aunt Julie, who cried out, "For goodness' sakes, child, look where you're going!"

Mary imagined saying to her: "I will be your mother, Bess, if you like. I will be your father's wife when he comes back, and together we will look after you."

But as the months passed and turned into a year, and then into a second, Mary Higson began to forget about Cy Bellman, and when a traveling salesman from Boston passing through Lewistown bought her a leather trunk and some clothes and many other things besides, she threw in her lot with him and left, and never again returned to Lewistown or found out what became of Cy Bellman and his little girl.

Meanwhile Sidney Lott was a foot taller than he'd been last summer and he walked to church most Sundays with Dorothy Wallace, who was fourteen years old and the daughter of the schoolmaster.

Aunt Julie said what a pretty girl Dorothy had turned into and she wouldn't be surprised if Sidney and Dorothy weren't a married pair a few years from now. What did Bess think of that?

Bess said she thought nothing of it. Bess said that was the last thing in the world she'd think of thinking about.

Sometimes the river was too low even for the boy to move the pirogue upstream against the sluggish current.

Bellman lashed it to his waist then, and splashed through the water and had the boy lead the horses along the bank, and pulled until his feet were so cold and his legs were so tired he couldn't go any further, and he called over his shoulder to the boy that they were stopping for the night.

There were moments during the days when he cried out in frustration. "Call yourself a river!" he'd shout, walloping the fly-pocked surface of the gray, slow-moving water with the flat of the pirogue's paddle. All day, every day, he kept his eyes peeled in the hope that one of the animals would at long last make an appearance, yet they saw nothing.

"I am beginning to think," he said aloud to the boy one day, "that sluggish and low and lacking in water as it is, this river is likely the problem as far as the big beasts are concerned."

He splashed forwards a few more paces and then he stopped and nodded.

"Yes, I'm coming to the conclusion that, like cats, they have a great dislike of rivers, of streams and creeks and waterways of any kind."

None of their looping excursions into the hinterland close to the river had yielded anything stranger than a few unfamiliar grasses and flowers, the fat, spiny creature that looked like a species of prickly fruit with a tail; the large rabbits, the ugly trousered birds.

"None of our diversions away from the river have been long enough," he announced decisively to the boy, his habit of talking to him being quite entrenched now.

For a long time he sat with his compass. The two captains and their party had continued into the northwest; he and the boy would do differently.

"Come," he said.

They strike a course away from the river.

They travel southwest for a distance of three hundred and fifty miles. They come to another river, which one, Bellman at this point has no idea. They cross it, and he hopes the Indian remembers the way back, that he has some special part of his brain that memorizes such things, perhaps via the soles of his feet.

He is in much better cheer now. After that little wobble in the river, his enthusiasm is restored. In the evenings he stretches himself out contentedly in his coat after another long day's traveling and enjoys a little smoke of his pipe, writes to Bess. There is something endlessly pleasant about the quick flurries of bats in the trees at this time of day, and the soft crepitation of insects all around: a steady in-out susurration as if the earth itself is breathing. He does worry a little about snakes, it's true, and bears, and the wolves he hears howling sometimes in the night. But on the whole he rarely dwells on those fears, and, as far as everything that might lie ahead is concerned, he remains much more excited than anxious, and more full of optimism than any kind of dread. He's convinced he's right in thinking that his mistake so far has been to hug the river too closely, and that now he has corrected that mistake, things will soon be looking up. He still has a small supply of oddments in the tin chest to exchange for food, should the need arise, with any savages they come upon, and fingers crossed, those savages will be of the curious, childlike sort and not the ferocious, slave-taking variety. He is low on powder and ammunition, but as long as the boy does the lion's share of the hunting, he reckons they will manage for a while.

He calls the boy "Old Woman" now, in a bantering, affectionate way.

There are times when he thinks, What if I bring him back with me when we have accomplished our mission? Another helper around the place with Elmer? What would Julie have to say about that? Bellman chuckles, trying to picture his sister's face.

A day comes when Bess is sitting on the steps of the Lewistown subscription library waiting for her aunt Julie to finish a meeting with the minister and Helen Lott about a new window for the church.

When she looks up, it is the man in the yellow vest with the eyeglasses, from last time, telling her that it is within his power to waive the nine-shilling subscription if she would like to come inside.

"Thank you," says Bess, and she goes in.

The librarian shows her the big tomes of the President's expedition and brings her to a chair and a table.

She reads. She pictures her father on his journey: a small and lonely figure in a vast, empty land, making his way slowly along a wide, meandering river. She turns the pages of the captains' journals, conscious of her deficiencies when it comes to understanding everything they've written; the pages are full of words she's never seen before and cannot begin to decipher. But there are the maps and the sketches, and it is a joy to leaf through and look at these, and she is grateful for the words she *does* know—*long, short, safe, dangerous, hungry, difficult, beautiful, dark, light, old, new,* and a store of a good many others. She's grateful that when at last her father's letters do begin to come, she will be able to read whatever simple messages they contain.

The only thing she doesn't like is the fat man in the eyeglasses, the way his breath shudders next to her face when he bends to open one of the volumes and then, for what seems like a long time, turns the pages for her; the experience both unpleasant and bewildering. Bess knows she wants his breathing to stop, and yet she isn't sure if the fault is his for doing it, or hers for not wanting to put up with it. He is being kind to her; he is letting her see the books without paying the nine-shilling subscription. Perhaps he always breathes in that shuddering way close to people's faces. Perhaps he can't help it, perhaps it's because he's bending down in a slightly uncomfortable position; perhaps it would be disrespectful and ungrateful to pull away. So Bess holds herself very still and doesn't pull away, not even an inch, in case the librarian decides she's being rude and snatches the book back. For what seems like a long time she reads with him bending over her, only wishing that he wasn't there and that he would leave her, and, eventually, he does.

Eventually he returns to his long desk out in the vestibule by the front doors and Bess is able to remain in the library's reading room in peace.

Whenever she can, she returns. Whenever her aunt Julie is busy with the minister or Mrs. Lott or some sick person, Bess is back and turning the pages of the big books of the expedition, until one afternoon, with the sun pouring in through the tall glass windows, she falls asleep with her cheek on one of the volumes of the great journey.

She smells him before she even opens her eyes, a fusty reek of old cloth and some other kind of human or animal smell she cannot name or put her finger on though she thinks she has smelled it before. Her cheek is hot and has the wrinkled print of the page on it because in falling asleep she has crumpled it a little and also, she sees to her horror, dribbled a little on it. Her heart pounds and she is afraid of what the fat man is going to do now, that he will shout at her in front of all the other patrons for spoiling the precious book and then tell her to leave and never come back. Instead he leans towards her. He has another book between his fingers; he is holding it gently and sets it beside her face.

"Here," he says. "A children's book."

There are pictures of a man on a winged horse and a woman with a head of snakes; stories about a one-eyed giant and a man with a golden harp who descends beneath the ground to retrieve his beloved.

When she is leaving—Aunt Julie will be finished now, making her way from the Lotts' house to the library—he asks her if she liked the new book.

"Yes."

He has more, he says, in a special room if she would like to come. Bess hesitates before the door, thinking of the treasures behind it, but he is close to her now with his funny smell and his shuddering breath, closer than a person would ordinarily be, it seems to her, and when they step into the dark, she feels his hand on her bottom. Runs.

After this she is more wary of Elmer Jackson, who some weeks ago traced a circle with his thumb on her hand while her aunt Julie's back was turned. After today, and the librarian, she feels certain that before long Elmer Jackson is also going to try to put his hand on her bottom.

She becomes fearful, skittish. The world is harder to enjoy;

she feels anxious and afraid. She wishes her father would come home and that her mother had not died. "You have Aunt Julie," she tries to tell herself, but Aunt Julie does not seem like someone who will protect her. Aunt Julie is always inviting Elmer Jackson into the house and making him dinner and cups of coffee, or off having meetings with the minister or taking plates of food to sick people or paying calls on Sidney Lott's mother, Helen. "I am twelve years old," says Bess aloud to herself. "I am too young to be without any kind of protector."

She begins to let herself dream that her father is on his way home, that he will be here very soon.

She begins to let herself dream that he is no longer very far away.

She begins to let herself dream that while he's been gone he has managed to find not only the big monsters he was looking for but also her mother.

Like the man with the golden harp, he will bring her with him, except he will be cleverer than the man with the golden harp and not look back, he will keep going all the way until they are both home. She will look out from the porch and they will be coming towards her along the stony path in front of the house and they will stay and they will look after her and keep her safe from the man with the eyeglasses and Elmer Jackson.

Bess has no memory at all of her mother.

Her thimble and her knitting needles used to sit in a drawer in the square pine table. Small wooden knobs decorated the blunt ends of the needles, which were long and slender and cold. Bess has a pair of stockings made with them, and she can see how the neat stitches were produced by them, the empty spaces created by the needles. The stockings are no longer big enough for her feet, but she wears them sometimes on her hands around the house in winter when it's very cold in the mornings and the stove hasn't got properly started.

Mostly, though, she knows her dead mother from her striped blouse, which used to hang on the back of the door in her father's bedroom, behind his own Sunday shirt and the black pants he wore into Lewistown. For as long as she can remember, she has been curious about her, and more and more there are times when she hopes what the minister and her aunt Julie say is true: that she lives now in another realm. A realm with a narrow gate and many mansions, with springs of living water and no scorching heat and no more night. She asked her father once if what the minister and her aunt Julie said was true and her mother was living now in another realm, and he said, "Oh, Bess, I don't know," but there was a flat look in his eyes and it was a very long time since he'd gone with them to church and she was fairly sure that what he meant was that she wasn't.

Even so, Bess thought about it often, this other realm, and sometimes in the mornings between dreaming and waking it seemed to merge into the picture she had in her mind of the west, where her father had gone, which she imagined to be a place of undulating grass and blue skies and distant, craggy mountains, a place where things that were dead here in Pennsylvania and Kentucky were still alive.

There were times when Bess let herself consider the possibility that her father had taken her mother's blouse not so he could trade it with the Indians, but so that her mother would have something beautiful to wear when he found her; that the knitting needles and the copper thimble were so she'd have something to do on the long journey home.

What Devereux, the fur trader, remembered now was that he had promised to send on the letters.

"Of course," he recalled saying—the sight of the ill-favored Indian boy nudging his memory now, and reminding him of what he had promised: that he would be sure to send on the letters.

He would give them to the other trader, Mr. Hollinghurst, he'd said, when he went east in a month's time. Mr. Hollinghurst would take them as far as St. Charles and see about forwarding them from there.

"Thank you," the man had said. "You're very kind."

What, now, had been his name? Bowman? Bowper? Belper?

A big, lumbering man with a large rectangular beard who had passed through last spring. A black stovepipe hat on top of his thick red hair.

No, not Belper. Bellman. Yes.

His name had been Bellman.

The letters were for his daughter, he'd said, who was ten years old, no, eleven, and living for the time being, while he was away, in the care of his sister, who could be sharp but when it came down to it was a good woman who deserved his appreciation.

Devereux recalled asking the man what brought him so far from home, business or pleasure? The man had paused for a moment, as if he wasn't sure what answer to give, and then he'd described himself as "a kind of explorer."

A kind of explorer!

Was he hoping, Devereux had inquired with a wink, to prove the President's expedition wrong and discover a convenient river they had managed to overlook? Was it his aim to find a neat and tidy water passage that would avoid the mountains and take him and anyone else who wished to get there all the way to the Pacific Ocean?

The red-haired man had laughed softly and shaken his head. He'd laid a large and deprecating hand across his chest. No, no, nothing like that—though, as it happened, he had perused the journals of the President's expedition and it was his belief that there were certain large things the two intrepid captains and their men might have missed.

Devereux looked now at the Indian.

He was wearing the man's brown wool coat and his black stovepipe hat, and beneath the coat he had on what looked like a woman's pink and white blouse. There was no sign of his brown horse, and he was leading the man's black one. There were ribbons in his hair and strings of beads around his neck in various colors. A bell and a copper thimble hung from one of his ears, and, from what the fur trader could see, he had Bellman's two guns, his hatchet, his knife, his rolled blanket, his large tin chest, his various bags and bundles.

Until this moment Devereux had all but forgotten the mad red-haired adventurer.

Only the sight of the boy riding into the trading post now, wearing the man's clothes and leading his horse, recalled their meeting.

He'd hardly thought of Bellman since the morning he'd left—the bowlegged Shawnee boy trotting off behind him loaded up with buffalo meat and dried fish and a big stash of those little cakes made of roots the Indians made, which Devereux himself didn't much care for but which were always useful in an emergency.

He lifted his musket now to the height of his shoulder and pressed it into the boy's cheek, plucked Bellman's hat from his ribboned head and set it on the ground, and motioned with his boot for the boy to open the bags and the tin box and show him the other remnants of Bellman's escapade. He pushed the musket barrel harder into the boy's face.

"What happened?"

Way back when he'd been traveling alone along the Missouri River, there'd been the Spanish friar he'd told about his journey, what he was looking for.

The thin, half-bald monk had listened and nodded as Bellman recounted what was known about the bones and what wasn't: that they were likely rather old; that they were of an enormous size; that they appeared to belong to a species of gigantic beast no one had ever seen; that it seemed possible to some, himself included, that such a beast might be wandering about in the large, vacant places beyond the Mississippi.

The friar's rough, pale garment hung to his ankles above bare feet. His hands were small and brown with short, dirty nails. His face was very pleasant, his expression calm and kindly. He was looking off into the distance at the long and almost imperceptible westerly curve of the river.

"You will find them," he'd said with quiet conviction. "God would never suffer any of His creatures to be annihilated. Our globe and every part and particle of it came out of the hand of its Creator as perfect as He intended it should be, and will continue in exactly the same state until its final dissolution."

Bellman hadn't known what to say.

It was easy to mock people for their religion, and it seemed impolite, not to say ungrateful given the friar's promise to carry a bundle of letters for Bess with him when he returned to St. Louis, to disagree.

He hadn't liked to say that he wasn't inclined to believe a word of the friar's argument—that he didn't think anyone or anything, and that included the giant animals, had God to thank for their being or their not-being.

It had seemed discourteous to explain that it was a long time since he'd set foot in any sort of church; that for years now on a Sunday he'd walked his sister and his daughter to the door and left them there.

There had been a silence between them. You could hear the rhythmic slosh of the current against the low wooden parapet of the mackinaw as the oarsmen dug into the water and heaved them laboriously upriver.

Perhaps the friar had sensed Bellman's discomfort, his lack of belief even. He'd said he'd be sure to leave the letters at the post office in St. Louis when he got there.

"Thank you," Bellman had said.

It seemed a long time ago now, his meeting with the friar, a distant event that belonged, almost, to another world. He reckoned they'd traveled more than a thousand miles since, he and the boy; maybe a little more.

Together, since leaving Devereux, they'd endured every kind of weather, every variety of landscape and terrain. That first spring, when they'd begun to follow the river north and west—a few weeks of clear skies and warm breezes, and then nothing but endless rain. Nothing but water pouring down over the boy's black hair and Bellman's great sponge of a coat and the wasted, greasy-looking withers of the horses; the boy unrolling a pair of leggings and a tunic to clothe his gnarly, half-naked body; the two of them proceeding often on foot because it was too cold to ride for long.

Summer then, with swarms of midges and biting flies and mosquitoes and hard, baked ground that was like a giant's bed of nails, hammered into fist-sized lumps by the feet of a million buffalo. Long days riding and on foot under the hot sun, the boy in his skirtlet again, Bellman's big shadow and the boy's small, crooked one, the looming shapes of the horses. Bellman's stockings long ago worn away to nothing, his feet inside his holed boots puffy and gray like old, wet newspaper.

Winter, and long days when they scoured the landscape till nightfall for something to eat, no living things growing on the shrubs or the trees, when they ate bark and roots and sometimes a bullfrog dug out by the boy from the frozen mud.

Bellman tore shreds from his shirt and tied the scraps of cloth to trees, hoping to signal their presence to any natives who were there in the wilderness but too timid to show themselves. Devereux had told him to do this: that the cloth would reassure the savages that Bellman did not mean to harm them, and would entice them also, to come and see what goods might be on offer. More often than not, no one came, and Bellman regretted the loss of so many pieces of his shirt, but there were times when a small band crept out from the trees, a few men and several women, children. Old Woman From A Distance would hang back then, watching Bellman and the unfamiliar natives as they went about their business—the natives chattering away in their own particular language, Bellman displaying his guns to keep them in check, offering a little tobacco or a metal file in exchange for an armful of cakes or some fish; the boy wary and guarded, as if there was no one in the entire world he trusted but himself; the proceedings always coming to an end with Bellman drawing one of the big monsters in the earth—his idea of them, with their tall legs and their tusks, his arms flung out and pointing at the treetops to denote their great size, his wanting to know if the Indians were at all familiar with what he'd shown them. Their blank looks; their melting away again, back into the forest, and, after that, a freezing skin of snow all the time on Bellman's face and the boy's, sleet in an icy cape on top of their shoulders and the backs of the horses, on the roped pile of Bellman's goods; Bellman reluctant in such cold to tear off even the smallest shreds of his clothing.

Mostly they walked. The horses' feet, bruised by hidden rocks and the stumps of trees, were worn to the quick. The boy made hide coverings, which the animals wore like two short pairs of matching yellowish stockings, fore and aft.

And then spring again and a new river, and more fish, suddenly, than Bellman and the boy could eat, the boy catching them and drying them and pounding what they didn't eat and packing it into the bags; the two of them on their way again until one fine morning Bellman left their camp to wash himself and his clothes in the river—stripping, and dunking what remained of his worn-out shirt and his long johns and his trousers in the water, rubbing the tattered, foul-smelling garments over the stones.

"Old Woman!" he called through the trees, back towards their camp. "Come!"

It was so good to feel clean. On more than one occasion in

the course of their long journey he had tried to coax the boy into washing his handkerchief, which was the only piece of linen he possessed, and kept tucked into his leather waistband, but he would not be parted from it. Still, Bellman felt sure the boy would like to wash himself today, here in this new river on this fresh spring morning.

"Come!" he called out again into the trees, but Old Woman From A Distance did not appear, and when Bellman returned to their camp, naked and with water dripping from his hair and his beard, the boy was seated on a large stone and he was wearing Bellman's hat.

Bellman stopped a short distance away and set down his bundle of soggy clothing. He lifted a schoolmistressy finger.

"No," he said sternly. "Definitely, no."

He snatched the hat angrily from the boy's head and placed it firmly on his own.

He reached out and roughly lifted the boy's various necklaces and shook them so they rattled. He pulled on the ribbons in his hair, the piece of mirror glass that dangled from his ear.

"*Yours,*" he said loudly.

He pointed at the incredibly dirty white handkerchief the boy wore tucked into the waist of the skimpy garment that covered his private parts.

"*Also yours.*"

Then he gestured around their camp at the black horse and the brown horse, at the tin chest and his wet, just-washed clothes, at the blanket they'd forgotten that day they'd gone over the falls and which he occasionally lent to the boy when it was very cold, at all his other bags and bundles. He touched the brim of his hat with his large fingers.

"Mine."

He took his knife from the belt in his wet trousers and gathered up his hatchet and his guns and his coat with the metal inkwell pinned to the collar, and brought them all in a big, brimming armful close to the boy's face.

"Mine too," he said quietly. "Understand?"

He stooped so his big bearded face was level with the boy's. "Can you say, 'Yes I understand'? Can you?" He cupped a large hand behind his ear in an exaggerated fashion.

"Yours. Mine. Yes?"—still cupping his ear theatrically, waiting for an answer.

The boy was silent and Bellman shook his head. "I have a mind, Old Woman, to call this Camp Disappointment."

The boy stood, silent. He looked back at Bellman with cold, dark eyes, and Bellman had no idea what he was thinking.

For the whole of the rest of the day the boy avoided Bellman's gaze, and this was the start of Bellman worrying that Old Woman From A Distance was no longer happy to be there under the terms of their bargain; that he wanted more.

That evening when they ate, Bellman gave the boy a slightly larger share of what they had than he was used to.

"We will put today behind us," he said with a series of gestures he hoped, along with his conciliatory tone, explained his meaning. "We will forget it ever happened."

He held out a small piece of mirror glass and one of Elsie's knitting needles. "Here. You may have these."

The boy's hands closed around them, and Bellman nodded.

In Carter's, Bellman's sister Julie stood trying to decide between a pair of brown stockings and a pair of navy blue ones. Both were more expensive than any item of clothing she'd ever bought, and she had never in her whole life worn a pair of stockings she had not made herself. But she'd become aware, lately, of the stockings of other women, like Helen Lott, and the schoolteacher's wife. She'd become aware that they did not fall in wrinkles around the tops of their boots like her own.

In the end she chose the brown.

Carter wrapped them in paper and gave her a questioning look she ignored and told him she'd take a pound of apricots also.

Tonight there would be apricot pie for Elmer Jackson when he was finished in the yard.

She'd begun to look at him differently since Cy left, and he'd been coming almost daily to the house, the two of them together at the table in the evenings after Bess had gone to bed.

Elsie's ring was sewn into her skirt pocket. It didn't seem wrong to think of it now as hers.

The whole thing amazed her; something she'd always expected that had never happened.

Meanwhile in Lewistown that summer the librarian took delivery of four new brass lamps with green glass shades for the reading room. A new portrait of the President arrived too, from Harrisburg, in a black oak frame, which, with the help of Carter's youngest boy from across the street, he hung on the wall in the vestibule opposite the front doors.

He saw the little girl often through the library windows with her tight-lipped aunt and the slovenly yard hand who seemed to accompany the two of them more and more, these days, whenever they came into town.

She was still hungry, he was certain, for anything connected with her father's journey. You could see it in the way she'd perched on the edge of the tall chair and traced the words and maps on the pages of the journals with her finger, her mouth a little open.

What he'd found would interest her, he was sure.

It was there in one of the old gazettes: a short item about the big Kentucky fossils that included, beneath the commentary, a sketch. A sketch of how the creatures—if all the assorted lumps and fragments could be assembled into one entire skeleton and clothed in some appropriate skin or fur— might look.

It was a comical sight, so comical he'd shown it to his wife: a thing somewhere between an enormous wild boar and a very fat horse with tiny ears like a rodent's or a sheep's, and a pair of drooping, backward-curving tusks.

He thought it was unlikely, after the last time, that the girl would come back to the library.

In the past, though, he'd always found that one failure didn't necessarily mean the end of something. Other opportunities presented themselves eventually, you just had to be alert to them, and he had his class at the church now, for the children—the minister appreciative of his help; it seemed possible that she might attend at some point in the future and join him in the back room with the other children while the minister and the adult members of the congregation like his wife and her aunt conducted their business.

He kept the sketch of the ridiculous monster in the inside pocket of his vest. At the right moment, he would show it to her; give her a little, and promise her more.

He was becoming afraid that he would never find them. That they were not out here after all. That whatever mystery surrounded their disappearance was buried in the briny, sulfurous ground in the east with that shipwreck of tusks and bones he'd read about in the newspaper; that whatever the mystery was, he would not uncover it.

There'd been a few brief moments, not long ago, when he was sure they'd come upon them at last—a big, sudden movement up ahead, a frantic disturbance in the trees, branches being pulled and snapped, a spray of twigs, a swishing and a tossing and a noisy kind of chomping.

He'd signed to the boy to stop, put his fingers to his lips, his heart beating very fast, all the trees tossing their leaves and branches, timber falling, and then—oh.

Only the wind.

Only thunder rolling in, and lashing rain, and in the distance lightning: a spectacle of crackling white light in the darkening sky.

He began to feel that he might have broken his life on this journey, that he should have stayed at home with the small and the familiar instead of being out here with the large and the unknown.

There were times now when he would stop and look around at the fantastical rocks and shivering grasses and wonder how it was possible that he was standing in such a place. There were times when steam rose up in twisting plumes from beneath the earth; when the lush plains around them shimmered and swam beneath the sculpted rocks like the ocean.

One morning after they'd set off he stopped after only a few paces, overcome by the watery twinkling of the emptiness ahead. "Sometimes, Old Woman," he said softly, "I feel I am all at sea."

The intermittent appearance of natives now, though he'd come by this time to expect it, amazed him: the presence of people in the vast wilderness around them. Even though he was used to the rhythm of their journey—that he and the boy could travel for a month and see no one, and then without warning encounter a large camp, or a group of savages walking or fishing. Noisy children and men whose bodies gleamed with grease and coal, women loaded like mules with bundles of buffalo meat. A whole mass of them together, undifferentiated and strange, and present suddenly amidst the coarse grass and the trees, the rocks and the river, beneath the enormous sky. All of them wanting to touch his red hair. Half of them enthralled by his compass, the other half trying to examine his knife and the contents of his tin chest. All of them fearful of his guns and eager to traffic a little raw meat for some of his treasures.

More and more often, he found himself thinking of his own squat three-room house and fenced-in paddock, the stony track in front, Elmer Jackson's scruffy shack to the east beyond the maple copse, the Lotts' fine brick place and Julie's small, neat home, which she had closed up to come and look after Bess, a little to the north. He thought of the path into town. The short main street with its shops and taverns, with Carter's store and the library, the church and the minister's house. He pictured all the people he knew, going about their lives there.

To encourage himself to press on, he thought of his favorite story from the journals of the President's expedition: that the older of the two officers, Captain Clark, had brought with him a black servant: a stout, well-made Negro named York. So fascinated were the Indians by York's extraordinary person, so eager were they to touch his coal-colored skin and short, mossy hair to see if he was real, so desirous were they of being near him, that the expedition worried for his safety, fearing the natives might try to steal him. In the event, their curiosity, their wonderment, was so great, they did something else: they sent one of their women to lie with him, because they were very anxious to have at least one partly black infant of their own—some lasting memorial of his actually having been amongst them.

Bellman loved this story, felt strengthened by it—the notion that whatever your own idea of the known world, there were always things outside it you hadn't dreamed of.

He watched the boy, riding up ahead, and wondered if he had ever seen a black human, in his time with Devereux or before, and if not, what he would do if he came upon one. If he would reach for his bow, or hide in terror beneath the nearest cottonwood tree, or stick his finger in his mouth and touch the black skin to see if the paint came off.

At night, in the firelight, he watched the shadows come and go across the boy's illuminated face, which seemed to him to be both young and very ancient and thought, What is it like to be you? He felt again the dizzying weight of all the mystery of the earth and everything in it and beyond it. He felt the resurgence of his curiosity and his yearning, and at the same time felt more and more afraid that he would never find what he'd come for, that the monsters, after all, might not be here.

With his finger he traced the pattern of flowers that wound its way around the circumference of Elsie's thimble, round like the world, and wished himself home again. He rubbed the dull, greening metal with his thumb and closed his eyes and thought of Bess and wished; opened his eyes to the treeless desert he had come to and the boy moving around their camp, tidying up and hovering over the kettle on the fire.

He tried to smother his doubts. To continue to think of the huge beasts and ask himself questions about them as they went along.

Were they mild or fierce?

Solitary or sociable?

Did they mate for life?

Did they reproduce easily or with difficulty?

Did they care for their young?

But these last thoughts, when they came, produced a pang now, an ache, and as the months passed since he'd left the fur trader's camp with the Indian boy and they'd continued west, he found himself thinking less and less about the enormous creatures, and more and more about Bess. He found himself worrying that if he carried on much further, he might never make it home; he found himself wondering if his search for the vanished monsters might not turn out to have been undertaken at too high a price.

"You did *what*?"

Elsie's voice came to him sometimes and he found himself trying to explain himself—why it had seemed so important to him to come and why it had not seemed a terrible thing at the time to leave Bess for so long.

When he lay at night in his coat across the fire from the boy, he thought about his little girl and saw pictures of her behind his closed eyes—Bess being born; Bess petting her favorite jenny on the nose and whispering into its long ears; Bess waving like a windmill to him from the porch the day he left.

How long will you be gone?

A year at least. Maybe two.

In two years I will be twelve.

Twelve, yes.

He wondered how tall she would be now, if she was putting up all right with Julie, and if anything interesting or important had happened in her life since he left; if she was thinking yet of making a sweetheart of her friend Sidney Lott, or if she was still a tad young for that; if the letters had reached her safely. He wrote to her more and more often, every week and sometimes more, telling her he was doing well and making progress, that he hoped it would not be long now, that he would come upon the animals soon, and after that he would be on his way home.

The going was hard though. For long stretches there was no game and hardly any timber. Bellman and Old Woman From A Distance went hungry and had no fire at night. They walked through bearded grass and thistles ten feet high, through narrow gorges where rocky cliffs oppressed them on either side. All around them the country was barren and desert. It glittered with coal and salt.

Some days, for something to do, Bess took the hinny with the white splash on its forehead off down the stony track and along the creek. Sometimes she rode and sometimes she walked with the animal alongside. Today she rode and went until they came to the edge of the maple trees between the Bellman house and pasture and Elmer Jackson's shack in the distance on the south side of the creek. She could see his cow in front of the low lean-to he called a barn.

Suddenly the hinny stopped and would go no further.

Bess twitched the stick against the hinny's haunch and said, "Yip yip," but the hinny still wouldn't move.

"What is it?"

Bess shielded her eyes with her hand and looked off into the trees.

For a minute she sat on the hinny, and from the trees Elmer Jackson looked out. He wondered if this might be his chance. He took a few steps forwards but was, truth be told, a little wary of the hinny. It was the most recalcitrant of all Bellman's animals, more bad-tempered even than the molly mule they'd sold last season. More than once he'd seen it land a smart three-hundred-and-sixty-degree kick in the backside of its least favorite horse.

He watched Bess turn the ill-tempered beast around, and soon after that she was gone.

Jackson swallowed.

He wasn't sure how to manage it, or where.

Soon though, soon.

With a series of slow, deliberate gestures, the boy communicated to Bellman one morning that if they didn't reach the mountains in good time they would have to stop and wait till spring. They were still a long way off and if they started over them too late, the snow would come and there would be no pasture for the horses and then the horses would die and so would they.

Bellman tried to picture what the mountains would look like—a long, unbroken spine of craggy peaks, spiking the huge sky.

He was in an agony of indecision: whether to carry on with his quest or give it up as a bad job and turn himself around and begin the long trek home.

He didn't think he wanted another winter out here. He could not imagine waking to find the water in his kettle frozen like a white rock. He couldn't imagine traveling with an icy crust over everything they wore, on top of their horses and covering all his bags and bundles. He couldn't imagine the squeak of hooves in snow.

Also, he'd had another thought.

What if they hibernated?

It seemed more than possible to him that the huge animals might be the sort to hibernate—that they might want to find themselves some warm and suitably roomy burrow in which, like the bear, they might hole up until the weather improved.

Which would mean waiting till next spring before any possibility of seeing them. It would mean plodding through the snow or building some sort of semipermanent camp and crossing his fingers that he and the boy would be able to feed themselves. He had already trudged through two long and drifty winters since leaving home, and he wasn't sure if he could face another.

They had stumbled upon another river, and for the time being they were following it.

It seemed to be taking them west, so even if the big beasts were giving the water a wide berth, Bellman reasoned it was possible the river would take them most quickly to some habitat they favored.

Winter. It still seemed a world away. The heat thickened and the mosquitoes were a torment. Bellman found himself wishing they hadn't dumped the pirogue when they'd struck away from the Missouri. He'd give anything now to squeeze into the narrow craft behind the boy while Old Woman From A Distance paddled them along.

They ate pounded fish and bulbs the boy harvested with his feet from the bottoms of pools. Bellman, still fearful he might leave, gave him a string of blue beads and two bells and Elsie's copper thimble and her other knitting needle.

After several weeks, the banks on both sides of the river began to shrink almost to nothing, narrow strips of ground, and towering cliffs walled them in on either side. They splashed through the water, leading the horses. Then the cliffs beside the river receded and the ground flattened out and they rode beside it. When Bellman was too sore to ride he staggered on weak legs in his worn-out boots over the cooked, hard earth.

And then he got sick.

The pounded fish made him vomit, the smallest quantity left him bent in spasms. His shit was a terrible white, crumbly and dry. He could no longer hunt. The boy did everything. He used his bow as he'd always done, but he also used the two guns, and he had the knife now too, and the hatchet, both tucked into the waist of his skirtlet. He did all the skinning, cut up all the meat, even sharpened the two knitting needles and used them to scrape out the marrow from the bones.

Bellman's flesh began to melt away, and one morning he woke on an island in the middle of the river where Old Woman From A Distance had made their camp. Fine sand blew from the sandbars and was driven in such clouds Bellman could hardly see. He lay looking through swollen, abraded eyes at the movement of the willows against the sky and could not get up.

He was conscious of the boy moving around the camp—could feel his presence like a soft shadow.

What is it like, to be you? he thought, watching the boy as he went about his tasks.

Bellman remembered wanting to ask the boy the same question once before, months and months and months ago, and it came back to him now from that time. Had he asked him, in fact, back then? Had he spoken the question aloud? He may have, he wasn't sure.

✦

If he had, and the boy had understood it, how would he have answered it?

Hard to say.

The boy is, after all, only eighteen years old. A mess of feelings.

You could say that he is angry about the past, but ambitious for the future. Impossible to say which impulse will turn out to be the stronger, or if the two things are simply bound together in him and inseparable; the essence of who he is.

Perhaps the truest thing you can say is that everything he does, he hopes it will be for the best.

They stayed there a week, and towards evening on the seventh day the boy brought a squirrel. He cooked it in Bellman's kettle and shredded it with his fingers and dropped threads of meat into Bellman's blackened mouth, but Bellman retched and choked.

That night Cy Bellman lay thinking about the long way he'd come.

Of all his various encounters, one kept returning to him: his meeting on one of the bateaux with the Dutch land agent who'd agreed to take some of his letters to St. Louis. Bellman had told him about his quest, and had used the same words he'd read in the newspaper: "I am seeking a creature entirely unknown," he'd said, "an animal incognitum."

He knew the words only because they'd been in the newspaper, and he wondered now if he'd sounded very pompous, very self-important. Perhaps he had. Anyway, the Dutchman must have told his wife about their conversation, because when the time came for Bellman to jump off the big flat boat and continue on his way, she'd called after him to say she hoped he'd reach Cognitum before nightfall, that he wouldn't lose his way before he got there, and as he rode away, he'd heard her high, trilling laughter.

Had he made a mistake, coming to America in the first place? Dragging Elsie halfway across the world so she could die in an unfamiliar place? Should he have stayed in England, in the narrow lanes and what now seemed like the miniature hills of his youth, everything small and dark and cramped and a feeling inside himself that he would burst if he did not escape? Even then, a little of that prickling feeling, the vertigo; a longing for what he'd never seen and didn't know.

The boy wore Elsie's blouse now; most of the bits and pieces Bellman had brought in the tin chest, and in the two bags, he'd given away to the boy because he was afraid that without them the boy might not stay. Nearly all the things Bellman had brought with him the boy had now, including all his weapons.

Bellman felt himself getting weaker, more and more he wasn't sure if he was awake or dreaming. He seemed to have forgotten the purpose of his journey. What had tormented him in his own small house no longer assailed his mind. The possibility of the enormous creatures disturbed neither his days nor his nights. What he thought about now was home; Bess.

At the height of his fever he could feel the slow, hot waves of his blood, beating against something inside him. Against what? His life? Against the things that had happened in it? Against all the things he had and hadn't done? Was that what he could feel inside himself?

He remembered the moment of his daughter's birth, the pulse of Elsie's body, the terrible limbo when it seemed that between them they would not manage this last part—getting Bess born; when she'd been suspended, half out in the world and half stuck, still, inside Elsie's body, balanced between life and death, and then the great sluicing suck and pull and she was out, bawling and alive.

He recalled her childhood illnesses—her pale skin besieged by crusty spots, her swollen throat, a cough that sounded like a wild animal's, a strawberry tongue, covered with little bumps, the creases in her skin red—red in the folds of her elbows and the lines of her neck. Nights when they thought she might not see the morning. What had Elsie done then? There'd been cold water and there'd been hot, but he couldn't remember why. What he knew for certain was that Elsie had sat and often put her hand on Bess's forehead and left it there, a steady weight.

He slept and woke and slept again, sang old songs he'd crooned to Bess when she was a soft parcel against his shoulder. His vision was dark, there were shadows and small clouds of moving color he thought must be sunlight, and trees, and Old Woman From A Distance.

Perhaps Julie was right. Perhaps he should do something sensible with his time, and though he did not think he could go back to church, perhaps he could find himself a new wife. Julie had mentioned Mary Higson, the blacksmith's widow, more than once. Perhaps when he got back he should marry Mary Higson, a mother for Bess, the three of them a family; make a better go of the mules, enough money to take on Elmer Jackson full-time. In a few years, perhaps, move a little further west to some nice fertile spot like the ones he'd passed through before crossing the Mississippi. Branch out into some cereal farming.

You had so many ways of deciding which way to live your life. It made his head spin to think of them. It hurt his heart to think that he had decided on the wrong way.

A thing seemed important until there was something more important.

He looked at himself in one of the remaining fragments of mirror glass he had in the tin chest and laughed. He'd need to clean himself up a bit. Visit the barber for a bath and shave his mustache, cut his beard, which was dirty and long and large enough to hide a small bird.

He could only lie on the ground now and occasionally open his eyes. Pictures of his faraway house, of his tall and bony sister standing stiff and protective with her hand on Bess's shoulder, floated before him. In fits and starts he talked. At one point he looked at the guns slung across the boy's chest, at his hickory bow and the stone-tipped arrows he always carried in a pouch around his neck, and although he knew the boy could not understand, he told him that he himself had always been more of a worrier than a warrior, and then laughed a little at his own joke. Loose, separate thoughts flocked and scattered in his brain. Once, he said aloud that he thought there must be a pattern to things but he could not see it. After that he didn't speak again, and Old Woman From A Distance could not wake him. When he touched him, his skin was sometimes hot and sometimes cold, and the boy thought the thing to do now was to make a warm pit so that when the man woke he could step down into it and stand, and breathe in the smoke and the warmth and it would revive him. He had seen it work, in the course of his life, many times, but in the event Bellman came to only slightly, only enough to sit up and have his right arm lifted over the boy's narrow, sloping shoulder and be half-carried down into the pit, where he did not have the strength to stand, and since in the boy's way of doing things it was important for Bellman to be upright if it was all to work, Bellman leaned propped up against him, crumpled and, like the boy, very thin. Their collarbones clicked against each other and Bellman's head drooped and rested in the shallow cradle of the boy's neck. Bellman's red beard touched the boy's face and the boy found that he did not mind. He no longer associated the big explorer with the skinny white man from the past. For an hour or so the fire breathed smoke inside the pit, and it seemed possible for a while that it would work, but at the end of an hour Old Woman From A Distance felt the life go out of Bellman and he was alone.

"You'll be needing a new dress," said Aunt Julie, "in the spring."

They would get the cloth at Carter's, she said, something tough and serviceable, and she would show Bess how to cut out the pieces and put them together. In the meantime, Bess could let down the hem on the present one, which was patched and darned and a hand's width too short now that the top of Bess's head came up past the height of the old wall clock.

Bess sat at the table in her shift. There was a dark line, crusty with grit, where the old hem had been. She cleared out the crud with her fingers and pressed the material flat and sewed up the new hem as far beneath the line as it was possible to do.

"And take the brush," Aunt Julie called from the porch, "to that dirt from when you were lying down in it yesterday."

All through the previous afternoon Bess had stayed in the back, stretched out on the damp, lumpy ground watching a snail make its slow, stubborn way through the stiff grass and over stones and fallen leaves and rotted branches; its meandering, silvery trail, the way it seemed to know, somehow, where it was going and how to get there.

She finished the hem with a knot and bit off the thread. The dirt from yesterday she left and put her dress back on and went outside.

Every day now she collected the eggs Aunt Julie's hens left

in the coop and in the pasture and in their favorite hiding places behind the house.

Most mornings the eggs were what she and her aunt ate, and once a week they took the ones they had left over into town, where Carter bought them, or exchanged them for oil or string or salt or sometimes a bag of fruit if Aunt Julie was making one of her pies.

It was harder than before, living with her aunt Julie, because although Bess didn't like her any more than she ever had, she felt the need to stay close to her these days. She felt safer when her aunt was nearby; glad that she was always in the house when Elmer Jackson came.

Then one morning Aunt Julie said the new colored window for the church had arrived by ship all the way from Banff in Scotland.

It had crossed the Atlantic Ocean and traveled in a wooden frame on a wagon over ground from the coast.

There would be a small welcoming party to receive it, she told Bess, but no children—the colored panes would depict Moses Blazing with Light, and it would be a terrible thing if they had come all this way, only to be smashed into a thousand pieces by an unruly infant.

"I am not an infant, Aunt Julie."

"No, Bess, but you are still a child and the minister has said no persons under fifteen years old." She said she expected to be back before dark, but if it all ran on and she was delayed, Bess was to leave her supper on the table under a cloth and not wait up. At the end of the track she joined Helen Lott and her husband, Gardiner, and together they began the long walk to the church.

✦

Elmer Jackson watched Julie go.

He gave it a couple of hours, in case the aunt decided she'd forgotten something and turned herself around and came back. After that he put on his hat, and went over there; stopped at the gate into the pasture to make sure it was shut because he had a weird kind of inkling that maybe the hinny the girl was so fond of—the one with the violent, unpredictable kick and the white splash on its forehead—would find some way of interfering. He tugged on the rope that was there to secure the gate and, satisfied that it was doing its job, turned and began to walk up to the house.

He had lit a fire and dug a pit, the boy told Devereux. He had held the white man in his arms and let him breathe in the smoke but he had died anyway.

He had buried the big leather saddle with him, along with his boots and a quantity of unused paper, because it seemed important to put him in the ground with something of his own.

Everything else, as the fur trader could see, he'd brought back with him: the knife, the hatchet, the two guns, a metal file, the brown wool coat, the fishhooks and the remaining tobacco, the tin box with what was left of its treasure, the tall black hat, the blanket, the kettle, the two leather bags, the satchel with its long buckled strap, the papers with drawings on them and the ones with the same repeated thing on them that was like two hills together and an eye and two snakes exactly the same, which he liked and considered because of its frequent repetition to be of some significance.

BessBessBessBessBessBessBessBessBessBessBessBessBessBess

He had also kept the dead man's black, brown-tailed horse. His own he'd traded for food on the journey back home because for a long time there'd been no game and no fish. Devereux saw that he had the small ink container too, which had been stuck through the lapel of the man's coat; he was wearing it behind his ear, like a flower.

The fur trader nudged the musket deeper into the boy's cheek. He didn't know what to believe. He stepped on the boy's hand and heard the bones crunch. The boy yelped.

"Tell me the truth now. Did you kill him?"

"No."

Everything, said the boy, had happened exactly as he'd described.

Devereux grunted.

He leafed through Bellman's surviving papers—his drawings of grasses and flowers and trees, the occasional bird or creature. A jackrabbit, a horned frog, some sort of vulture. There were dried specimens between the pages, notes written in a series of cramped, misspelled sentences, various sketches with the dotted lines of his route. Letters to the daughter. No indication whatever that he had come upon the mammoth creatures he was seeking.

Devereux pictured again the red-haired man's large, earnest features, the thick rectangular beard, and was moved.

He recalled the serious way Bellman had spoken of the great beasts, and his mission to find them, and found himself strangely touched by the news of his death. The letters were full of mad hope and a kind of deranged curiosity, the last few telling the daughter that he expected to find the animals very shortly and then to be on his way home. It would be good to see her, the letters said. He hoped her aunt Julie was well, and that Elmer Jackson was not proving himself too troublesome a neighbor.

The fur trader sat down with the pile of notes and drawings and surveyed the things that remained of the man's demented quest. Some of the letters to the daughter were loose, numbered sheets with the girl's name on the first page. Others were already folded into fat squares, tied and knotted with cord, and on the front, in Bellman's large handwriting, a few lines describing the whereabouts of his house in the United States. It all produced in the trader's mind a picture of the little girl waiting for her father to come home, the crusty old sister who was perhaps softer on the inside than she was on the out. He recalled the letters that he had promised to send and then forgotten about.

Well, he would send them on now to St. Charles with these new ones, along with the notes and the drawings, with Hollinghurst when he left.

He told the boy he could go—he could keep the blouse and the red beads for his trouble. The coat and the pretty copper thimble he could take off and leave with everything else here in a pile next to the dead man's hat.

The boy stared back truculently and didn't move.

He said the dead man's things were his, for all the services he had rendered.

Devereux passed a hand across his face and sighed.

No, he said, they were not. The things were in his custody now, all except the letters and the drawings, which he would send with Mr. Hollinghurst, who was going east, as it happened, in the morning. Mr. Hollinghurst would do his best to see they got back to the daughter.

The boy stuck out his bottom lip. He seemed very aggrieved. He took a step forward. He said if Devereux let him keep the tin box of treasure, and one of the two guns and the hatchet, and the dead man's tall hat and his coat and the metal flower with the spike, he would go instead of Mr. Hollinghurst. He could find his way if it was described to him. He would take all the papers and give them to the girl.

Devereux sucked his teeth.

He felt guilty about not sending on the letters, he did. His mother would have called it a sin of omission, and he wished now to put it right. Nevertheless, he also had a commercial eye on the gear the bandy-legged Indian had brought back. He was already totting up the number of dark, glossy pelts he'd have in exchange for it by the end of the week.

"No," he said.

He told the boy he had no need of his services for this one. Mr. Hollinghurst would do what needed to be done. "Now go away. Shoo."

But the boy didn't move.

He said he'd do it for less. He'd do it for one of the guns and the blue beads and the blouse and the coat and the tall black hat.

Oh, these people, thought Devereux.

Was there anything they wouldn't do in exchange for a clapped-out weapon and some fancy dress and a handful of glittery trash?

He looked at the boy, at his sloping shoulders and his dark, piplike eyes, at his ribbons and his beads and the grimy woman's blouse, which he said had been given to him by the dead man for helping him on his journey. He was thinner than before and very dirty, and there was something unspeakably tawdry and undignified about him being dressed in the old cotton blouse. A small piece of mirror glass hung from the end of one of his pigtails next to the copper thimble. Knotted around the other was the now filthy handkerchief Devereux recalled Bellman giving him at the start of everything.

Devereux hesitated.

Oh, what the heck.

There was, perhaps, an advantage in the boy going. He had enough about him to make Devereux think he might be a better option than any arrangement made in St. Charles by Hollinghurst—the letters misdirected or given to the wrong person or left behind and forgotten for a second time—and he didn't want that to happen, he really didn't. He felt bad about not sending on Bellman's letters in the spring as he'd promised. It was just possible the boy might make a more reliable courier than Hollinghurst.

"All right, here's the deal."

The boy could have the dead man's coat if he went, and the last of his treasure—the bits of copper wire and the remaining handkerchiefs and the mirror glass, one of the knitting needles but not both of them, and all the remaining white and red beads but not the blue ones, and Devereux would throw in a carrot of tobacco and a tot of rum. And he could keep the blouse.

The boy did not respond. He stood. He seemed to be turning the proposal over in his mind. He said he'd do it if he could have one of the guns too.

Devereux shook his head. "No."

The hat then, said the boy.

Ah, the hat!

The fur trader eyed the boy narrowly, wondering if he'd waited to ask for the hat because it was the thing he wanted most.

"You can have the hat when you get back. And the gun." The older of the two guns along with the hat would be his on his return.

"Entendu?"

The boy looked at his feet. "Entendu," he said quietly. *Agreed*. It was one of his few French words.

Then, using the back of one of the dead man's drawings and the ink in the little container that had been behind the boy's ear, Devereux wrote to Bess, in English.

He said he hoped the return of her father's letters and papers would be a comfort.

He told her to be sure to send her own scrap of writing back with the Indian to show she had received them.

"So I know you went there," he said to the boy, looking up at him as he wrote his message to Bess. "So I know you didn't just ditch the man's letters in the river and run off with all this booty here." He handed his letter for Bess to the boy and watched him place it in the bag with the other letters.

"Mr. Hollinghurst is leaving tomorrow for St. Charles," he said. "You can accompany him, and from St. Charles, Mr. Hollinghurst will indicate how you are to go the rest of the way." He paused. "You can take the man's compass." Devereux stooped and picked the small, plum-sized ebony thing out of the tin chest and put it into the boy's hand, explaining the work it did and tapping the important spot he must follow in relation to the arrow.

"It is not a gift," he said. "It is a loan and I'll be having it back when you return with the piece of paper from the girl."

The narrow-shouldered Indian turned the compass over in his hand. Devereux could not tell if he considered it useful or not. Still, the boy's fingers closed around it and he gathered up the miscellaneous items Devereux said were his for making the journey east to deliver the letters and the papers to the

dead man's daughter. Devereux saw him cast one last, covet-
ous look at the hat and the gun, which were promised to him
on his return, and then Mr. Hollinghurst came, and after that
they were gone, the two of them heading off on their horses
in an easterly direction.

Ah well, it was worth a try. Devereux reckoned he had a
fifty-fifty chance of ever seeing the boy again.

n St. Louis he smelled beer and whiskey and flour and molten iron. It was the noisiest and most crowded place he'd ever seen. St. Charles, when they got to it, was quieter, but it still frightened him, the idea of being alone in it.

He had no warm feelings at all for Mr. Hollinghurst, who in the years that he'd known him had been even stingier than Devereux and always struck him much harder when he was angry. Even so, he was sorry when Mr. Hollinghurst turned to him in St. Charles and said, "I'll be leaving you now, so listen up while I tell you how to go."

Like Devereux, he always spoke to the boy in the boy's own language.

"This," said Hollinghurst, stamping down on the ground with his boot, "is *here*."

He spoke slowly and loudly, as if to a stupid child. "Now, give me the green ribbon from your hair and that long string of blue beads you have there and your short string of white ones."

When he hesitated, Hollinghurst rolled his eyes and turned irritable. "Don't worry, I am only borrowing them to show you the way you need to go and then I will give them back. Now, give."

He watched the fur trader's long fingers arrange the things he had given him on the ground so that the blue beads trailed away from the toe of his boot and the white ones led off from the end of the blue ones and the green ribbon made a separate squiggle further along. "So. First you'll take yourself along the Ohio River here"—Hollinghurst pointed to the blue beads—"which will bring you into Pennsylvania. Then you'll carry on along the Allegheny and then along Mahoning Creek"—the white beads—"and when you reach the mountains you'll hop over to the western branch of the Susquehanna River"—the green ribbon—"then head south, and here, further on"—he tapped a spot beneath the ribbon with his toe—"is your dead man's house."

The trader told him the things to look for, the shapes of the big mountains he would come to before the Susquehanna River, and of certain hills and forests beside the rivers, and the occasional appearance of groups of brick and wooden buildings, the likely position of the dead man's place in a valley beyond a medium-sized town.

The boy nodded. He was ashamed he didn't know the territory himself; that he had no memory of it.

Mr. Hollinghurst said he would expect to see him back at the trading post well before the beginning of winter. "All right?"

"All right," said the boy.

For a long time before St. Louis and St. Charles, as he'd traveled with Mr. Hollinghurst, there'd been people who looked like him. Along the smaller rivers they'd come upon them all the time, hustling for toll money or goods in exchange for allowing them to cross where they wanted to, in the least difficult places. Just before they got to St. Charles, a whole band had clattered by on horses, wrapped up in their red blankets, and for a while after that there'd been camps and villages. Now, as he made his way further and further east, as he passed over the mountains and through broad valleys, there seemed to be none at all.

He rode without a saddle, mostly at night, the fur trader having told him he would not be welcome where he was going. Across his chest on a strap he wore his various necklaces, his small hickory bow, and a hide pouch on a strap containing his arrows and the papers.

"I am in a different world," he said to himself.

Even in the darkness he was anxious about being seen. When he saw a light, or the blacker shape of a house up ahead, and heard the huffing of cattle or the yapping of dogs or any sound suggesting occupation or settlement of any kind, he made a large, looping arc around it. The weather was good. What little rain there was fell during the day, while he slept, or in brief showers. Slowly, day by day and night by night and week by week, he made his way east.

The compass the fur trader had given him he had no use for because he had the music of the river and the bright configuration of the stars, but he carried it in his hand because he liked it for its beauty and the suspicion that it had some secret power of its own the fur trader wasn't telling him about; that it was alive in some way. He liked the way the tiny needle quivered beneath the clear covering, like his own heart when he was out stalking or waiting with a hook for a fish to bite.

The dead man's papers shifted and crackled against his chest as he went along. There were moments when he seemed to see him again, scribbling away—the dip of the point of one of his half-bald feathers into the ink, the sound that was like the working of the claws of a small creature on a leaf or the smooth bark of a tree.

They belonged to the daughter now, the fur trader had said, and the boy was pleased he had no need of them or any desire to possess them because it meant he would not mind giving them up. It was true that he liked the pictures—the drawings of the trees and flowers and grasses—and the pattern of marks with the sideways hills and the eyes and the snakes, which Devereux said signified the name of the dead man's daughter. That was striking and pleasing too. But he did not desire any of the papers in the way he desired the gun or the tin box or the hat or the blouse. He was still angry with Devereux for keeping so much of the dead man's booty for himself and as he rode east he wondered if the stingy fur trader had any intention at all of ever giving him the beautiful hat. He thought about this a great deal as he went on mile after mile in the darkness of the night. He could always try, perhaps, to hold on to the compass; if Devereux tried to keep the hat then he could refuse to give back the compass.

The land he passed through was soft and fertile. There was wheat and hemp and cotton and every sort of fruit.

He came to several towns that were smaller than St. Charles but had all the things he'd seen in St. Charles, with many houses, taverns, mills, churches, farms. Even in the dark when he skirted them, he could tell that the places were busy and full of people. All the buildings were made of wood or brick and sometimes stone. Large and solid. Then forests and cultivated fields and lots of hills, then more towns and farmhouses and roads. Then sometimes for long stretches, nothing—a log cabin, one large house. Cows, sheep, hogs. From behind one large house he took vegetables and a chicken. Mostly though he hunted and picked what he found. The wind blew from the west and was very soft. On the roads there were wagons full of people and baggage. A lot of the time the traveling was very rough because the horse stumbled on long stretches of limestone. Beside him lofty banks covered with trees and shrubbery rose up beside the river.

When he came out of the mountains along the Susquehanna there was a half-built bridge and from his hiding place he saw people cross on a flatboat poled by four men. He waited in the pine trees. It was dark and foggy. He waited till night, then crossed the river himself with the water up to his shoulders, the horse lifting in the swift current and swimming.

After the bridge, more houses and taverns and mills and churches and farms.

He thought often about the dead white man, and how he too had been stingy like the fur trader to begin with, then less so after the day he shouted at him for trying on the tall hat. It had been a good time, after that, the big explorer rewarding him every so often with some small, new item as they traveled through the rain and the roasting heat towards the setting sun in pursuit of the fabulous animals.

For a long time after he began his journey back towards Devereux alone, Old Woman From A Distance had missed Bellman, plodding forwards on his big, booted feet, or up on the black horse, rocking from side to side, the squeaks and creaks of his leather saddle, dipping his pen into the ink in his coat and, more and more towards the end, stopping suddenly as they went along to sit without moving, as if he couldn't think what he was doing or how he'd come to be where he was; at night playing with the little copper ornament and in his sleep twitching and murmuring.

Old Woman From A Distance still missed the cracked, quiet singing that had come near the end, and there were days just before the dawn when he crept into the trees and tethered his horse and curled up in the leaves, and tried to recall it.

He thought about the dead man's dusty drawings.

The four legs like giant trees, the monstrous bodies and vast curving tusks. It was true what he'd told Devereux, that he'd never seen anything like the creature the man had sketched in the dirt.

He'd heard about them though.

For as long as he could remember he'd heard stories about the vast man-eating creatures: his people had seen their bones when they lived in the east, sunk in the soft, briny clay of a wooded valley. The very same ones, perhaps, that the big red-haired explorer had read about. But what he'd been told was that the monsters were all gone—that they'd vanished forever when the Great Spirit, the Big God, had destroyed the huge bloodthirsty animals with thunder and lightning because the beasts had preyed upon his people, consumed them.

Which begged the question, why did the Great Spirit not destroy the white settlers from across the sea the way He'd destroyed the mammoth animals?

He'd asked his father the very same question the day they'd packed up their things and begun to move out of the east, and his father had shrugged. He'd said the world was full of mysteries and you had to be patient, and for now all he could say was that they had fought and they had lost and the best thing they could do was to leave with the things they'd been given.

In the darkness he continued along narrow paths and bad roads over hills and rocks, old trees and rivers, through clouds of insects. If there were any remnants of his people or others like them, living quietly still in the forests, he did not see them.

He thought about his sister, and the settlers, and about the things which had been half of what his people had been promised by the government for leaving their lands in the east and agreeing to move off into the west. He thought about the old man also, from those times when he was a boy: his warnings against entering into any kind of commerce with any white men, his prophecy that if they did, it would be the beginning of their end.

Old Woman From A Distance still wasn't sure what to think.

One thing he was sure of though: there was no Great Spirit. No Big Man in the Sky looking out for them. If there had been once, there wasn't anymore.

He liked the dead man's horse very much. It was a nicer color than his old one and it went faster. Sometimes, to encourage himself, he laid his mouth against its soft, leaflike ears and whispered, "Remember, there are no gods. We have ourselves and nothing else."

As he headed east he felt the pleasing heaviness of the dead man's coat around his shoulders, the soft and beautifully striped blouse lifting in the breeze. He thought of the tall hat and the gun that would be his, as long as the fur trader did not cheat him, if he delivered the letters to the girl. It did not feel wrong to want any of these things. He was small and his name was not a fine one, but riding along now on the dead

white man's excellent horse, wearing his gear and with more
to come, he did not feel like any kind of fool. He felt grand
and purposeful. He felt intelligent and adventurous. He felt
like someone on a mission that made him different from other
people.

The journey east, though, was long and difficult.

In the daytime, while he hid in the forests, he slept, and
when he woke in the dusk and there was still a little light, he
took out the dead man's letters. He liked the crackle of the
pages, the drawings of trees and grasses and animals. It was
annoying he could not read what they said. He turned them
over, these dry, patterned things, and wondered what mysteries they contained. He would have liked it if Devereux or Mr.
Hollinghurst had taught him to read. He would have liked it
if they'd instructed him in both their languages, but they had
always spoken to him in his own tongue. They seemed to want
to keep their own languages a secret, a pair of weapons they
did not want to give away.

In his time with the dead man, the boy could tell that the
language he spoke was more or less the same as Mr. Hollinghurst's. The big explorer had spoken often and loudly in
this language, as if he expected one day that the boy would be
able to understand it all, but Old Woman From A Distance
had understood almost nothing of the words themselves,
only a handful here and there, familiar from Mr. Hollinghurst. He could tell when the big man was angry or sorry or
excited or uncertain, but the little scrapings he possessed of
the man's language were not enough to make sense of him,
and there was nothing at all that helped him to understand
what was written on the papers. The one thing he knew,

because Devereux had at least told him this: that the small, repeated picture at the tops of many of the papers signified the daughter.

Old Woman From A Distance did not recognize the country from his childhood. It was no more than dimly familiar, remote and far-off, like something half-felt in a dream which had slipped away the moment he'd woken. The fresh, varied greens of the summer trees, the dark green-blue of the river, the slight sinking into the rich earth of his horse beneath him each time they took a step forwards in the direction he'd been told to go—all these things seemed to belong to a world that had shifted somehow and been reshaped between the roads and the buildings and the fields he passed so that he could no longer decipher it.

It had frightened him, what the fur trader said, that people would not be pleased to see him in places where they expected all his kind to have left. Hunting was difficult in the darkness, and he was very hungry. By the time he was nearly there, he had only one arrow left, the rest had gone off into the night in pursuit of a rustle or the crackling report of something good to eat and he had not found them again and then the last one he'd used up on a raccoon he'd seen slinking through the leaves, which had scampered away before he could catch it, the arrow stuck in its haunch, wagging in the gloaming and then gone and he had nothing now with which to kill his food or to defend himself. He was afraid of the white people, their guns. He wished he could have got one of the dead man's guns from Devereux. He loved guns. He felt very alone, the only company the small blue needle in the wooden case that quivered next to his heart.

BessBessBessBessBessBessBessBessBessBessBessBessBessBess

He looked at them now, the sideways hills, the half-closed eyes, the two small, wriggling snakes. No picture in his head of the girl herself. His dreams a jumble of everything: Devereux and Hollinghurst and the dead man and the dead man's daughter and the dead man's gear, the big bundles that were half what his people had been promised, the rivers and forests and gardens of his childhood, corn and beans and squash ripening in the sunshine, the skinny white settler who'd taken his sister, the old man's warnings. Hills, and eyes, and snakes, and everything else that had ever happened in his life and might yet happen in the future. Over and over and over.

Ever since the librarian, Bess had become more and more afraid of Elmer Jackson, and she wasn't sure what would happen now that she saw him coming, but she thought she had known for a while that sooner or later something would, it was only a matter of time.

He turned up regularly these days to carry out some small repair, or help Aunt Julie with the mules, but he'd never come before when Aunt Julie was absent, and the word *covering* came now into Bess's mind: a picture of what happened when the stallion came to cover the jennies and how sometimes the jennies ran away and Elmer Jackson had to go chasing after them to bring them back, and what happened then, and how afterwards the jennies mostly went to stand in the corner of the field with their heads lowered and looking miserable.

He had her pinned to the wall now with his arm across her throat.

He was breathing hard and fumbling with his belt buckle. A lumpy blood vessel, thick and awful, pulsed next to the cords of his neck. He stank of hinny crap and his own unclean clothing. She closed her eyes. A spurt of vomit filled her mouth.

She cried out for her aunt Julie even though she knew there must be no hope of being heard. Aunt Julie was a long way out of earshot and was not here to protect her. Aunt Julie would be in church by now, looking up at the stained glass beauty of Moses Blazing with Light.

Bess bit Jackson's chin and his cheek and clawed at his back and screamed, but his belt only clunked to the floor and his pants fell against her leg.

M r. Hollinghurst had described a narrow valley bordered by low, tree-covered hills, a creek to the north and then a town; the dead man's place a short ride beyond it along a stony path; a log house with a porch and a fenced pasture in which there would likely be mules. This, said Mr. Hollinghurst, was what was written on the front of the folded letters, and the boy did not think he could be far now.

For the first time in his long journey, feeling himself to be so close, he continued beyond daybreak instead of pausing to hide himself in the trees till nightfall, looping around the town's string of buildings and making his way through the trees back to the road that led away from them to the east.

He arrived at a white church and heard singing from within. Ahead he could see the stony path.

Perhaps it was the unaccustomed daylight that distracted him.

Perhaps it was because he was sleepy after traveling through the whole of the night and now through half the morning too.

Either way, he was caught off guard; didn't see the fat white man until he was almost upon him. Up ahead next to a tall shrub behind the church: a fat white man in a yellow vest and a pair of eyeglasses with his hand inside his trousers.

The boy hushed his horse and stepped her into the trees. He'd seen many white men before this one who'd produced pistols from inside their clothing. Had this one seen him? He wasn't sure.

The fat man glanced quickly to the left and right, and then his gaze seemed to fall in the boy's direction and he appeared to pause, as if on the brink of something. Old Woman From A Distance could see now that he was definitely holding something in his hidden hand. The boy's heart was beating very fast. "I have no weapon," he said to himself. "No arrows left, and no gun because that mean, chiseling fur trader Devereux wouldn't let me have one until I go back."

Which is when he remembers the knitting needle.

With a quick, tight knot he shortens the stretchy sinew of his small hickory bow, bites down hard into the soft wooden knob at the blunt end of the long steel needle till he has a groove; sets it in place, draws back his arm, and shoots the fat librarian dead.

Pleased and a little surprised by the accuracy of his shot, he dismounts. The knitting needle being a precious thing and because he doesn't know when he might need it next, he draws it out from the man's neck, which it has pierced like a maple trunk, the dark sap bubbling out over the man's vest and shirt and pants.

The boy regrets the lovely vest, which is the same beautiful color as his favorite flower. The eyeglasses he hesitates over, having no use for them himself, his own eyesight being quite extraordinarily sharp. But he is old enough and wise enough and experienced enough to know that the fact that something is of no use to him doesn't mean it is of no use to someone else and therefore valuable. And even if the eyeglasses turn out not to have any value as eyeglasses, the glass itself is surely too good to pass up, as are the thin pieces of curved metal around the man's spongy white ears.

He lifts them off and drops them into the pocket of Cy Bellman's big coat, wipes the knitting needle quickly on the sleeve of the dead man's shirt, gets back on his horse, and continues in what feels to him, from the position of the sun and the movement of the wind and the last details of Mr. Hollinghurst's instructions, like the right direction.

Bess holds her breath, and tells herself to think of something different. Something far away and nothing to do with the present moment and what is happening in it. Her only hope that it will soon be finished.

Out in the yard one of the jennies brayed. A loose shingle shifted somewhere up on the roof in the wind. Behind her the clock ticked loudly and the little ledge at the bottom of it dug into the back of her head as Jackson maneuvered her against the wall. She closed her eyes.

And then the boy remembers.

With the road and the small wooden town at his back, he pauses. The undulation of the hills, the configuration of the woods, the fresh scent of the summer grasses and the rich, dark earth—they all come back to him from his childhood, arriving across time on the breath of the morning wind.

"This was mine," he thinks, emerging from the maple copse. "I am here. I am back where I came from and where it all happened."

Grunting then, and moaning. Jackson bunching her dress in his fist, calling her his baby.

Then hoofbeats in the distance, and through the open door between Elmer Jackson's heaving shoulder and his damp red neck, a figure on a black horse approaching at a gallop down the long, stony track across the pasture from the west, a figure with dark, flying pigtails in a flapping brown coat and a billowing, pastel-colored blouse that looked to Bess like some undreamed-of holy trinity of her father, her mother, and some stranger she had never met in her entire life.

"Help me!"

She kicked and bit and clawed at Jackson's back.

For a long time the figure on the black horse seemed to come no nearer, and Jackson had her drawers off and her legs up around his waist. More hoofbeats then and some whinnying, a long, dusty-sounding skid, and something feather-light and swift launched through the clear morning air and glittering with a silvery light and coming out through Jackson's eye just in front of her nose.

She felt Jackson unstick and peel away from her and sink to the floor.

He twitched once, and then he was still.

The Indian was beardless and not tall, with narrow, slightly hunched shoulders, wearing her father's coat and her mother's blouse. Threaded in his dark braids, ribbons of various colors, around his neck strings of beads, blue and white and red, a small tinkling bell and a copper thimble she recognized beneath one of his ears.

She took a gulp of air.

Heavens. First Elmer Jackson. Now an Indian wearing her parents' clothes.

She was shaking, unable to speak.

Perhaps it was because of the two years she'd spent living with her aunt Julie, and because it was a long time now since she'd chattered away to Sidney Lott on a Sunday morning, that Bess, when she did speak at last, sounded more like a woman of forty-five than a girl of twelve and a half:

"Thank you, sir," she said, still catching her breath. "I am very much obliged to you for the timing of your arrival."

She couldn't tell if he understood. She thought probably not, since he only stood before her and said nothing. He was sweating from the ride, and his face gleamed. He was like no one she had ever seen.

Bess straightened her torn and rumpled clothing. She was trembling violently. She did not want to ask the boy how he came to be wearing the blouse and the coat and the thimble. She did not want to know how he had come to possess one of her mother's knitting needles or to be riding her father's horse. She did not want to know anything more than she knew now. She did not believe he was the bringer of good news.

The boy said nothing.

When he is old, he will still think sometimes of the man moving against her in the distance. Visible through the open door, like an animal through a tunnel of trees, illuminated in a surrounding darkness.

From a bundle on his horse he took out the papers that had been entrusted to him by the fur trader and gave them to her.

"Oh," said Bess.

There were the unsent letters, of course, with her name on them, and there were drawings of unfamiliar grasses and trees and shrubs, a few small, strange animals and birds, a large rabbit, and between the pages some pressed and crumbling leaves and tiny, dry seeds that fell across her hands.

There was the letter from Devereux explaining to her that her father had died and that his bones were buried in the west.

There were no drawings at all of any huge, tusked creatures.

"Excuse me, please, for a moment," she said to the boy and walked out onto the patched and sloping porch.

For a long time she stood shielding her eyes from the sun and looking off into the west, willing, in spite of the news the boy had brought, a tall figure in a stovepipe hat to appear through the settling dust and the small, pale rocks kicked up by the swift, black horse, but none came. There was the sky and the trees and the long path, and she could see that was all there was, but she still stood there and looked, her mind doing everything it could to avoid believing what it had been told; everything it could to refuse the news. Only her body accepted it with its violent trembling, and she fought, now, to overcome it, aware that she was poised before a flood, which, if she allowed it, would engulf her, and she would not be able to come up for air.

At the pine table she sat down and wrote to the fur trader as he'd asked. The boy held out his hand for the piece of paper and she gave it to him.

"You may keep the blouse," she said quietly, "and the coat and the thimble." It seemed a small price to pay for the services he had rendered, though again it was hard to tell if he understood.

In a louder, slower voice she said, "I will go to the pump and fetch us each a mug of water. We will both feel better for a cold drink I am sure. Stay here please, I will only be a minute."

Bess always wondered what the boy was thinking while she was away at the pump, what his feelings were beyond being, presumably, rather tired.

She wondered if he was afraid that someone would come after him because of Elmer Jackson lying there in a river of his own blood with a knitting needle through his face—if he believed she herself might even have gone to fetch such a person.

She wondered if, standing there in the strange house with the pale light of the morning all around, he'd found himself feeling suddenly very homesick or if there was some extremely pressing appointment, or person, he had to get back to in a hurry.

The only thing she was fairly certain about was that he must have felt he deserved more for his trouble than her mother's dirty blouse and her copper thimble, and her father's old, travel-worn coat, because when she returned from the pump with the two tin mugs of water, one for each of them, not only was he was gone—not only had he taken the hair on Elmer Jackson's head and retrieved the bloodied knitting needle from his eye and taken that too, along with Elmer Jackson's gray horse—he had also taken, from inside the house, the crocheted pot holder from its hook on the wall beside the range, a dish cloth, two forks, a knife, and a spoon, an embroidered apron, and her aunt Julie's black umbrella.

For a while she stood on the porch holding the mugs of water and looking off into the west, but there was no sign of him. The only evidence that he had ever come, other than the things he'd taken that were no longer in the house, was the body of Elmer Jackson lying beneath the clock.

She drank the water and waited until her heart had slowed a little.

Aunt Julie would be very cross about the pot holder and the dish cloth and the embroidered apron, and she would be furious about the cutlery and her umbrella, which had a silver ferrule and had only recently been repaired.

"Well," said Bess aloud, "I will say I went out with the john mule for wood, and that when I came back, the things were gone."

In the meantime she would fetch a bucket and scrub the blood from the floor and tie Elmer Jackson by his ankles to the hinny and drag him out into the far pasture, where the ground was soft and easy to dig, and she would dig a pit for him and roll him in, and cover it over.

Her father's letters she would keep under her mattress and she would not tell her aunt Julie about any of it, ever.

She did not wish for her aunt, or the Lotts, or anyone else in Mifflin County, to know that he had fulfilled their mean-spirited prophecies and not returned; that he had never found the enormous creatures he was seeking.

She did not want to hear what her aunt Julie would have to say about his failure.

She did not wish him to be named a fool, to be numbered amongst the lost and the mad.

Nor did she want to tell her aunt Julie about the smooth-faced Indian who had saved her and robbed them and then left without a word of goodbye.

It seemed likely that her aunt would find something bitter and disapproving to say about him too, and she preferred, therefore, to keep that part a secret also.

As for the compass, it wasn't clear to her if he had dropped it in his haste to be gone or if he had left it for her on purpose. Either way, she did not put it under her mattress but kept it in her pocket with her hand around it and continued to think of him riding away, back into the west. The bloodied knitting needle, she supposed, would be in his empty quiver with the cutlery, and he would be carrying the umbrella under his arm, like a lance. The pot holder he would have tied, perhaps, onto his head, the dish cloth and the embroidered apron around his shoulders. When she closed her eyes she saw them fluttering behind him in the morning breeze like a flag, and a jeweled cape.

ACKNOWLEDGMENTS

My very grateful thanks to the Dorothy and Lewis B. Cullman Center for Scholars and Writers at the New York Public Library for a 2016/17 Fellowship, which was so important to me in the writing of this book. Thank you to Jean Strouse and her wonderful team there, and to the curators and librarians at the NYPL.

Thank you to Salvatore Scibona, Akhil Sharma, and Jonathan Stevenson, who first read and commented on the manuscript.

Thank you to David Constantine, Cathy Galvin, Mary O'Donoghue, and Sophie Rochester.

To Marion Duvert and Anna Webber.

To Sarah Goldberg and Bella Lacey.

Special thanks to Bill Clegg.

And to Michael, always.

Keep in touch with
Granta Books:

Visit granta.com to discover more.

GRANTA